Also by Elie Wiesel

NIGHT

DAY (previously THE ACCIDENT)

THE TOWN BEYOND THE WALL

THE GATES OF THE FOREST

THE JEWS OF SILENCE

LEGENDS OF OUR TIME

A BEGGAR IN JERUSALEM

ONE GENERATION AFTER

SOULS ON FIRE

THE OATH

ANI MAAMIN (cantata)

ZALMEN, OR THE MADNESS OF GOD (play)

MESSENGERS OF GOD

A JEW TODAY

FOUR HASIDIC MASTERS

THE TRIAL OF GOD (play)

THE TESTAMENT

FIVE BIBLICAL PORTRAITS

SOMEWHERE A MASTER

THE GOLEM (illustrated by Mark Podwal)

THE FIFTH SON

AGAINST SILENCE (edited by Irving Abrahamson)

THE OSLO ADDRESS

TWILIGHT

THE SIX DAYS OF DESTRUCTION (with Albert Friedlander)

A JOURNEY INTO FAITH (conversations with John Cardinal O'Connor)

A SONG FOR HOPE (cantata)

FROM THE KINGDOM OF MEMORY

SAGES AND DREAMERS

THE FORGOTTEN

A PASSOVER HAGGADAH (illustrated by Mark Podwal)

ALL RIVERS RUN TO THE SEA

MEMOIR IN TWO VOICES (with François Mitterand)

KING SOLOMON AND HIS MAGIC RING (illustrated by Mark Podwal)

AND THE SEA IS NEVER FULL

THE JUDGES

CONVERSATIONS WITH ELIE WIESEL (with Richard D. Heffner)

WISE MEN AND THEIR TALES

THE TIME OF THE UPROOTED

Dawn

DAWN

ELIE WIESEL

TRANSLATED FROM THE FRENCH BY FRANCES FRENAYE

HILL AND WANG

A DIVISION OF FARRAR, STRAUS AND GIROUX

NEW YORK

Hill and Wang
A division of Farrar, Straus and Giroux
18 West 18th Street, New York 10011

Copyright © 1961, 2006 by Elie Wiesel
Translation copyright renewed © 1989 by Elie Wiesel
Preface copyright © 2006 by Elie Wiesel
All rights reserved
Distributed in Canada by Douglas & McIntyre Ltd.
Printed in the United States of America
Originally published in 1960 by Éditions du Seuil, France, as L'Aube
English translation originally published in 1961 in the United States by Hill and Wang
This paperback edition, 2006

Library of Congress Cataloging-in-Publication Data
Wiesel, Elie, 1928–
     [Aube. English]
     Dawn / Elie Wiesel ; translated from the French by Frances Frenaye.
       p.   cm.
     ISBN-13: 978-0-8090-3772-8 (pbk. : alk. paper)
     ISBN-10: 0-8090-3772-6 (pbk. : alk. paper)
     I. Frenaye, Frances, 1912–   II. Title.

PQ2683.I32A913 2006
843'.914—dc22

                                                    2006041063

Designed by Abby Kagan

www.fsgbooks.com

11   13   15   17   19   20   18   16   14   12   10

to François Mauriac

THIS NOVEL, MY FIRST, may be surprising for its sudden relevance to our present times. Does it not have to do with hostage-taking, violence, and clandestine rebellion?

Yet the action of the novel is set in a past at once recent and far away, in a Palestine that is still Jewish, ruled by Great Britain, before the creation of the state of Israel.

Elisha, a young survivor of the death camps—an orphan bereft not only of his father and mother, but of hope—is recruited by members of the Resistance. At this point the enemy is not Arab but English. The power is in London, not Jerusalem. The tribunals are overburdened, the prisons overflowing. The executioner is working full-time. His justice is draconian.

A Jewish combatant is condemned to death. His superiors in the Resistance order Elisha to execute one of His Majesty's officials in retaliation. Both men are to die at dawn.

Dawn is purely a work of fiction, but I wrote it to look at myself in a new way. Obviously I did not live this tale, but I was implicated in its ethical dilemma from the moment that I assumed my character's place. Difficult? Not really. Suppose the American army, instead of sending me to France, had handed me a visa to the Holy Land—would I have had the courage to join one of the movements that fought for the right of the Jewish people to form an independent state in their ancestral homeland? And if so, could I have gone all the way in my commitment and killed a man, a stranger? Would I have had the strength to claim him as my victim?

So I wrote this novel in order to explore distant memories and buried doubts: What would have become of me if I had spent not just one year in the camps, but two or four? If I had been appointed kapo? Could I have struck a friend? Humiliated an old man?

And taking the questions further within the context of the narrative: How are we ever to disarm evil and abolish death as a means to an end? How are we ever to break the cycle of violence and rage? Can terror coexist with justice? Does murder call for murder, despair for revenge? Can hate engender anything but hate?

The young hero spends an entire night preparing himself. He looks back on his blighted childhood, his open wounds. At the core of his being, he rejects the new part he is to play. He is afraid of betraying the dead who, as judges and witnesses, observe the living but are unable to come to their aid. And yet . . .

What will dawn bring for him? More darkness, or the light of the coming day?

This is where we see two men, albeit enemies, pursue a simple and inevitable dialogue illuminating the human truth that hatred is never an answer, and that death nullifies all answers. There is nothing sacred, nothing uplifting, in hatred or in death.

In this story, which calls religious and cultural ideas into question, I evoke the ultimate violence: murder. It aims to put on guard all of those who, in the name of their faith or of some ideal, commit cruel acts of terrorism against innocent victims.

And yet, this tale about despair becomes a story against despair.

—ELIE WIESEL

Dawn

S OMEWHERE A CHILD began to cry. In the house across the way an old woman closed the shutters. It was hot with all the heat of an autumn evening in Palestine.

Standing near the window I looked out at the transparent twilight whose descent made the city seem silent, motionless, unreal, and very far away. Tomorrow, I thought for the hundredth time, I shall kill a man, and I wondered if the crying child and the woman across the way knew.

I did not know the man. To my eyes he had no face; he did not even exist, for I knew nothing about him. I did not know whether he scratched his nose when he ate, whether he talked or kept quiet when he was making love, whether he gloried in his hate, whether he betrayed his wife or his God or his own future. All I knew was that he was an Englishman and my enemy. The two terms were synonymous.

"Don't torture yourself," said Gad in a low voice. "This is war."

His words were scarcely audible, and I was tempted to tell him to speak louder, because no one could possibly hear. The child's crying covered all other sounds. But I could not open my mouth, because I was thinking of the man who was doomed to die. Tomorrow, I said to myself, we shall be bound together for all eternity by the tie that binds a victim and his executioner.

"It's getting dark," said Gad. "Shall I put on the light?"

I shook my head. The darkness was not yet complete. As yet there was no face at the window to mark the exact moment when day changed into night.

A beggar had taught me, a long time ago, how to distinguish night from day. I met him one evening in my home town when I was saying my prayers in the overheated synagogue, a gaunt, shadowy fellow, dressed in shabby black clothes, with a look in his eyes that was not of this world. It was at the beginning of the war. I was twelve years old, my parents were still alive, and God still dwelt in our town.

"Are you a stranger?" I asked him.

"I'm not from around here," he said in a voice that seemed to listen rather than speak.

Beggars inspired me with mingled feelings of love and fear. I knew that I ought to be kind to them, for they might not be what they seemed. Hassidic literature tells us that a beggar may be the prophet Elijah in disguise, come to visit the earth and the hearts of men and to offer the reward of eternal life to those who treat him well. Nor is the prophet Elijah the only one to put on the garb of a beggar. The Angel of Death delights in frightening men in the same way. To do him wrong is more dangerous; he may take a man's life or his soul in return.

And so the stranger in the synagogue inspired me with fear. I asked him if he was hungry and he said no. I tried to find out if there was anything he wanted, but without success. I had an urge to do something for him, but did not know what.

The synagogue was empty and the candles had begun to burn low. We were quite alone, and I was overcome by increasing anxiety. I knew that I shouldn't be there with him at midnight, for that is the hour when the dead rise up from their graves and come to say their prayers. Anyone they find in the synagogue risks being carried away, for fear he betray their secret.

"Come to my house," I said to the beggar. "There you can find food to eat and a bed in which to sleep."

"I never sleep," he replied.

I was quite sure then that he was not a real beggar. I told him that I had to go home and he offered to keep me company. As we walked along the snow-covered streets he asked me if I was ever afraid of the dark.

"Yes, I am," I said. I wanted to add that I was afraid of him, too, but I felt he knew that already.

"You mustn't be afraid of the dark," he said, gently grasping my arm and making me shudder. "Night is purer than day; it is better for thinking and loving and dreaming. At night everything is more intense, more true. The echo of words that have been spoken during the day takes on a new and deeper meaning. The tragedy of man is that he doesn't know how to distinguish between day and night. He says things at night that should only be said by day."

He came to a halt in front of my house. I asked him again if he didn't want to come in, but he said no, he must be on his way. That's it, I thought; he's going back to the synagogue to welcome the dead.

"Listen," he said, digging his fingers into my arm. "I'm going to teach you the art of distinguishing between day and night. Always look at a window, and failing that look into the eyes of a man. If you see a face, any face, then you can be sure that night has succeeded day. For, believe me, night has a face."

Then, without giving me time to answer, he said good-by and disappeared into the snow.

Every evening since then I had made a point of standing near a window to witness the arrival of night. And every evening I saw a face outside. It was not always the same face, for no one night was like another. In the beginning I saw the face of the beggar. Then, after my father's death, I saw his face, with the eyes grown large with death and memory. Sometimes total strangers lent the night their tearful face or their forgotten smile. I knew nothing about them except that they were dead.

"Don't torture yourself in the dark," said Gad. "This is war."

I thought of the man I was to kill at dawn, and of the beggar. Suddenly I had an absurd thought: what if the beggar were the man I was to kill?

Outside, the twilight faded abruptly away as it so often does in the Middle East. The child was still crying, it seemed to me more plaintively than before. The city was like a ghost ship, noiselessly swallowed up by the darkness.

I looked out the window, where a shadowy face was taking shape out of the deep of the night. A sharp pain caught my throat. I could not take my eyes off the face. It was my own.

AN HOUR EARLIER Gad had told me the Old Man's decision. The execution was to take place, as executions always do, at dawn. His message was no surprise; like everyone else I was expecting it. Everyone in Palestine knew that the Movement always kept its word. And the English knew it too.

A month earlier one of our fighters, wounded during a terrorist operation, had been hauled in by the police and weapons had been found on him. A military tribunal had chosen to exact the penalty stipulated by martial law: death by hanging. This was the tenth death sentence the mandatory power in Palestine had imposed upon us. The Old Man decided that things had gone far enough; he was not going to allow the English to transform the Holy Land into a scaffold. And so he announced a new line of action—reprisals.

By means of posters and underground-radio broadcasts he issued a solemn warning: Do not hang David ben Moshe; his death will cost you dear. From now on, for the hanging of every Jewish fighter an English mother will mourn the death of her son. To add weight to his words the Old Man ordered us to take a hostage, preferably an army officer. Fate willed that our victim should be Captain John Dawson. He was out walking alone one night, and this made him an easy prey for our men were on the lookout for English officers who walked alone in the night.

John Dawson's kidnapping plunged the whole country into a state of nervous tension. The English army proclaimed a forty-eight-hour curfew, every house was searched, and hundreds of suspects were arrested. Tanks were stationed at the crossroads, machine guns set up on the rooftops, and barbed-wire barricades erected at the street corners. The whole of Palestine was one great prison, and within it there was another, smaller prison where the hostage was successfully hidden.

In a brief, horrifying proclamation the High Commissioner of Palestine announced that the entire population would be held responsible if His Majesty's Captain John Dawson were to be killed by the terrorists. Fear reigned, and the ugly word *pogrom* was on everyone's lips.

"Do you really think they'd do it?"

"Why not?"

"The English? Could the *English* ever organize a pogrom?"

"Why not?"

"They wouldn't dare."

"Why not?"

"World opinion wouldn't tolerate it."

ELIE WIESEL

"Why not? Just remember Hitler; world opinion tolerated him for quite some time."

The situation was grave. The Zionist leaders recommended prudence; they got in touch with the Old Man and begged him, for the sake of the nation, not to go too far: there was talk of vengeance, of a pogrom, and this meant that innocent men and women would have to pay.

The Old Man answered: If David ben Moshe is hanged, John Dawson must die. If the Movement were to give in the English would score a triumph. They would take it for a sign of weakness and impotence on our part, as if we were saying to them: Go ahead and hang all the young Jews who are holding out against you. No, the Movement cannot give in. Violence is the only language the English can understand. Man for man. Death for death.

Soon the whole world was alerted. The major newspapers of London, Paris, and New York headlined the story, with David ben Moshe sharing the honors, and a dozen special correspondents flew into Lydda. Once more Jerusalem was the center of the universe.

In London, John Dawson's mother paid a visit to the Colonial Office and requested a pardon for David ben Moshe, whose life was bound up with that of her son. With a grave smile the Secretary of State for Colonial Affairs told her: Have no fear. The Jews will never do it. You know how they are; they shout and cry and make a big fuss, but they are frightened by the meaning of their own words. Don't worry; your son isn't going to die.

The High Commissioner was less optimistic. He sent a cable to the Colonial Office, recommending clemency. Such a gesture, he said, would dispose world-wide public opinion in England's favor.

The Secretary personally telephoned his reply. The recommendation had been studied at a Cabinet meeting. Two members of the Cabinet had approved it, but the others said no. They alleged not only political reasons but the prestige of the Crown as well. A pardon would be interpreted as a sign of weakness; it might give ideas to young, self-styled idealists in other parts of the Empire. People would say: "In Palestine a group of terrorists has told Great Britain where to get off." And the Secretary added, on his own behalf: "We should be the laughingstock of the world. And think of the repercussions in the House of Commons. The opposition are waiting for just such a chance to sweep us away."

"So the answer is no?" asked the High Commissioner.

"It is."

"And what about John Dawson, sir?"

"They won't go through with it."

"Sir, I beg to disagree."

"You're entitled to your opinion."

A few hours later the official Jerusalem radio announced that David ben Moshe's execution would take place in the prison at Acre at dawn the next day. The condemned man's family had been authorized to pay him a farewell visit and the population was enjoined to remain calm.

After this came the other news of the day. At the United Nations a debate on Palestine was in the offing. In the Mediterranean two ships carrying illegal immigrants had been detained and the passengers taken to internment on Cyprus. An automobile accident at Natanya: one man dead, two injured. The weather forecast for the following day: warm, clear, visibility unlimited . . . We repeat the first bulletin: David ben Moshe, condemned to death for terroristic activities, will be hanged . . .

The announcer made no mention of John Dawson. But his anguished listeners knew. John Dawson, as well as David ben Moshe, would die. The Movement would keep its word.

"Who is to kill him?" I asked Gad.

"You are," he replied.

"Me?" I said, unable to believe my own ears.

"You," Gad repeated. "Those are the Old Man's orders."

I felt as if a fist had been thrust into my face. The earth yawned beneath my feet and I seemed to be falling into a bottomless pit, where existence was a nightmare.

"This is war," Gad was saying.

His voice sounded as if it came from very far away; I could barely hear it.

"This is war. Don't torture yourself."

"Tomorrow I shall kill a man," I said to myself, reeling in my fall. "I shall kill a man, tomorrow."

E LISHA IS MY NAME. At the time of this story I was eighteen years old. Gad had recruited me for the Movement and brought me to Palestine. He had made me into a terrorist.

I had met Gad in Paris, where I went, straight from Buchenwald, immediately after the war. When the Americans liberated Buchenwald they offered to send me home, but I rejected the offer. I didn't want to relive my childhood, to see our house in foreign hands. I knew that my parents were dead and my native town was occupied by the Russians. What was the use of going back? "No thanks," I said; "I don't want to go home."

"Then where do you want to go?"

I said I didn't know; it didn't really matter.

After staying on for five weeks in Buchenwald I was put aboard a train for Paris. France had offered me asylum, and as soon as I reached Paris a rescue committee sent me for a month to a youth camp in Normandy.

When I came back from Normandy the same organization got me a furnished room on the rue de Marois and gave me a grant which covered my living expenses and the cost of the French lessons which I took every day of the week except Saturday and Sunday from a gentleman with a mustache whose name I have forgotten. I wanted to master the language sufficiently to sign up for a philosophy course at the Sorbonne.

The study of philosophy attracted me because I wanted to understand the meaning of the events of which I had been the victim. In the concentration camp I had cried out in sorrow and anger against God and also against man, who seemed to have inherited only the cruelty of his creator. I was anxious to re-evaluate my revolt in an atmosphere of detachment, to view it in terms of the present.

So many questions obsessed me. Where is God to be found? In suffering or in rebellion? When is a man most truly a man? When he submits or when he refuses? Where does suffering lead him? To purification or to bestiality? Philosophy, I hoped, would give me an answer. It would free me from my memories, my doubts, my feeling of guilt. It would drive them away or at least bring them out in concrete form into the light of day. My purpose was to enroll at the Sorbonne and devote myself to this endeavor.

But I did nothing of the sort, and Gad was the one who caused me to abandon my original aim. If today I am only a question mark, he is responsible.

One evening there was a knock at my door. I went to open it, wondering who it could be. I had no friends or acquaintances in Paris and spent most of the time in my room, reading a book or sitting with my hand over my eyes, thinking about the past.

"I would like to talk with you."

The man who stood in the doorway was young, tall, and slender. Wearing a raincoat, he had the appearance of a detective or an adventurer.

"Come in," I said after he had already entered.

He didn't take off his coat. Silently he walked over to the table, picked up the few books that were there, riffled their pages, and then put them down. Then he turned to me.

"I know who you are," he said. "I know everything about you."

His face was tanned, expressive. His hair was unruly, one strand perpetually on his forehead. His mouth was hard, almost cruel; thus accentuating the kindness, the intensity, and warm intelligence in his eyes.

"You are more fortunate than I, for I know very little about myself."

A smile came to his lips. "I didn't come to talk about your past."

"The future," I answered, "is of limited interest to me."

He continued to smile.

"The future," he asked, "are you attached to it?"

I felt uneasy. I didn't understand him. The meaning of his questions escaped me. Something in him set me on edge. Perhaps it was the advantage of his superior knowledge, for he knew who I was, although I didn't even know his name. He looked at me with such familiarity, such expectation, that for a moment I thought he had mistaken me for someone else, that it wasn't me he had come to see.

"Who are you?" I asked. "What do you want with me?"

"I am Gad," he said in a resonant voice, as if he were uttering some cabalistic sentence which contained an answer to every question. He said "I am Gad" in the same way that Jehovah said "I am that I am."

"Very good," I said with mingled curiosity and fear. "Your name is Gad. Happy to know you. And now that you've introduced yourself, may I ask the purpose of your call? What do you want of me?"

His piercing eyes seemed to look straight through me. After several moments of this penetrating stare he said in a quite matter-of-fact way:

"I want you to give me your future."

Having been brought up in the Hassidic tradition I had heard strange stories about the Meshulah, the mysterious messenger of fate to whom nothing is impossible. His voice is such as to make a man tremble, for the message it brings is more powerful than either the bearer or the recipient. His every word seems to come from the absolute, the infinite, and its significance is at the same time fearful and fascinating. Gad is a Meshulah, I said to myself. It was not his physical appearance that gave me this impression, but rather what he said and the way he said it.

"Who are you?" I asked again, in terror.

Something told me that at the end of the road we were to travel together I should find another man, very much like myself, whom I should hate.

"I am a messenger," he said.

I felt myself grow pale. My premonition was correct. He was a messenger, a man sent by fate, to whom I could refuse nothing. I must sacrifice everything to him, even hope, if he asked it.

"You want my future?" I asked. "What will you do with it?"

He smiled again, but in a cold, distant manner, as one who possesses a power over men.

"I'll make it into an outcry," he said, and there was a strange light in his dark eyes. "An outcry first of despair and then of hope. And finally a shout of triumph."

I sat down on my bed, offering him the only chair in the room, but he remained standing. In the Hassidic legends the messenger is always portrayed standing, as if his body must at all times serve as a connecting link between heaven and earth. Standing thus, in a trench coat which seemed as if it had never been taken off and were an integral part of his body, with his head inclined toward his right shoulder and a fiery expression in his eyes, he proceeded to tell me about the Movement.

He smoked incessantly. But even when he paused to light a cigarette he continued to stare obliquely at me and never stopped talking. He talked until dawn, and I listened with my eyes and mind wide open. Just so I had listened as a child to the grizzled master who revealed to me the mysterious universe of the Cabala, where every idea is a story and every story, even one concerned with the life of a ghost, is a spark from eternity.

That night Gad told me about Palestine and the age-old Jewish dream of recreating an independent homeland, one where every human act would be free. He told me also of the Movement's desperate struggle with the English.

"The English government has sent a hundred thousand soldiers to maintain so-called order. We of the Movement are no more than a hundred strong, but we strike fear into their hearts. Do you understand what I am saying? We cause the English—yes, the English—to tremble!" The sparks in his dark eyes lit up the fear of a hundred thousand uniformed men.

This was the first story I had ever heard in which the Jews were not the ones to be afraid. Until this moment I had believed that the mission of the Jews was to represent the trembling of history rather than the wind which made it tremble.

"The paratroopers, the police dogs, the tanks, the planes, the tommy guns, the executioners—they are all afraid. The Holy Land has become, for them, a land of fear. They don't dare walk out on the streets at night, or look a young girl in the eye for fear that she may shoot them in the belly, or stroke the head of a child for fear that he may throw a hand grenade in their face. They dare neither to speak nor to be silent. They are afraid."

Hour after hour Gad spoke to me of the blue nights of Palestine, of their calm and serene beauty. You walk out in the evening with a woman, you tell her that she is beautiful and you love her, and twenty centuries hear what you are saying. But for the English the night holds no beauty. For them every night opens and shuts like a tomb. Every night two, three, a dozen soldiers are swallowed up by the darkness and never seen again.

✡ Then Gad told me the part he expected me to play. I was to give up everything and go with him to join the struggle. The Movement needed fresh recruits and reinforcements. It needed young men who were willing to offer it their futures. The sum of their futures would be the freedom of Israel, the future of Palestine.

It was the first time that I had heard of any of these things. My parents had not been Zionists. To me Zion was a sacred ideal, a Messianic hope, a prayer, a heartbeat, but not a place on the map or a political slogan, a cause for which men killed and died.

Gad's stories were utterly fascinating. I saw in him a prince of Jewish history, a legendary messenger sent by fate to awaken my imagination, to tell the people whose past was now their religion: Come, come; the future is waiting for you with open arms. From now on you will no longer be humiliated, persecuted, or even pitied. You will not be strangers encamped in an age and a place that are not yours. Come, brothers, come!

Gad stopped talking and went to look out the window at the approaching dawn. The shadows melted away and a pale, prematurely weary light the color of stagnant water invaded my small room.

"I accept your offer," I said.

I said it so softly that Gad seemed not to hear. He remained standing by the window and after a moment of silence turned around to say:

"Here is the dawn. In our land it is very different. Here the dawn is gray; in Palestine it is red like fire."

"I accept, Gad," I repeated.

"I heard you," he said, with a smile the color of the Paris dawn. "You'll be leaving in three weeks."

The autumn breeze blowing in through the window made me shiver. Three weeks, I reflected, before I plunge into the unknown. Perhaps my shiver was caused not so much by the breeze as by this reflection. I believe that even then unconsciously I knew that at the end of the road I was to travel with Gad, a man was waiting, a man who would be called upon to kill another man, myself.

Radio Jerusalem . . . Last-minute news flashes. David ben Moshe's execution will take place at dawn tomorrow. The High Commissioner has issued an appeal for calm. Curfew at nine o'clock. No one will be allowed on the streets. I repeat, no one will be allowed on the streets. The army has orders to shoot on sight . . .

The announcer's voice betrayed his emotion. As he said the name David ben Moshe there must have been tears in his eyes.

All over the world the young Jewish fighter was the hero of the day. All the wartime resistance movements of Europe held rallies in front of the British embassies; the chief rabbis of the capital cities sent a joint petition to His Majesty the King. Their telegram—with some thirty signatures at the bottom—ran: "Do not hang a young man whose only crime is fidelity to his ideal." A Jewish delegation was received at the White House and the President promised to intercede. That day the heart of humanity was one with that of David ben Moshe.

It was eight o'clock in the evening and completely dark. Gad switched on the light. Outside the child was still crying.

"The dirty dogs," said Gad; "they're going to hang him."

His face and hands were red and perspiring. He paced up and down the room, lighting one cigarette after another, only to throw each one away.

"They're going to hang him," he repeated. "The bastards!"

The news broadcast came to an end and a program of choral singing followed. I started to turn the radio off but Gad held me back.

"It's a quarter past eight," he said. "See if you can get our station."

I was too nervous to turn the dial.

"I'll find it," said Gad.

The broadcast had just begun. The announcer was a girl with a resonant, grave voice familiar to every one of us. Every evening at this hour men, women, and children paused in their work or play to listen to the vibrant, mysterious voice which always began with the same eight words: *You are listening to the Voice of Freedom* . . .

The Jews of Palestine loved this girl or young woman without knowing who she was. The English would have given anything to lay hands upon her. In their eyes she was as dangerous as the Old Man; she too was a part of the Legend. Only a very few people, no more than five, knew her identity, and Gad and I were among them. Her name was Ilana; she and Gad were in love and I was a friend to both of them. Their love was an essential part of my life. I needed to know that there was such a thing as love and that it brought smiles and joy in its wake.

You are listening to the Voice of Freedom, Ilana repeated.

Gad's dark face quivered. He was bent almost double over the radio, as if he wanted to touch with his hands and eyes the clear, deeply moving voice of Ilana, which tonight was his voice and mine and that of the whole country.

"Two men are preparing to meet death at dawn tomorrow," said Ilana, as if she were reading a passage from the Bible. "One of them deserves our admiration, the other our pity. Our brother and guide, David ben Moshe, knows why he is dying; John Dawson does not know. Both of them are vigorous and intelligent, on the threshold of life and happiness. They might have been friends, but now this can never be. At dawn tomorrow at the same hour, the same minute, they will die—but not together, for there is an abyss between them. David ben Moshe's death is meaningful; John Dawson's is not. David is a hero, John a victim . . ."

For twenty minutes Ilana went on talking. The last part of her broadcast was dedicated exclusively to John Dawson, because he had the greater need of comfort and consolation.

I knew neither David nor John, but I felt bound to them and their fates. It flashed across my mind that in speaking of John Dawson's imminent death Ilana was speaking of me also, since I was his killer. Who was to kill David ben Moshe? For a moment I had the impression that I was to kill both of them and all the other Johns and Davids on earth. I was the executioner. And I was eighteen years old. Eighteen years of searching and suffering, of study and rebellion, and they all added up to this. I wanted to understand the pure, unadulterated essence of human nature, the path to the understanding of man. I had sought after the truth, and here I was about to become a killer, a participant in the work of death and God. I went over to the mirror hanging on the wall and looked into my face. I almost cried out, for everywhere I saw my own eyes.

As a child I was afraid of death. I was not afraid to die, but every time I thought of death I shuddered.

"Death," Kalman, the grizzled master, told me, "is a being without arms or legs or mouth or head; it is all eyes. If ever you meet a creature with eyes everywhere, you can be sure that it is death."

Gad was still leaning over the radio.

"Look at me," I said, but he did not hear.

"John Dawson, you have a mother," Ilana was saying. "At this hour she must be crying, or eating her heart out in silent despair. She will not go to bed tonight. She will sit in a chair near the window, watch in hand, waiting for dawn. Her heart will skip a beat when yours stops beating forever. 'They've killed my son,' she will say. 'Those murderers!' But we are not murderers, Mrs. Dawson . . ."

"Look at me, Gad," I repeated.

He raised his eyes, shot me a glance, shrugged his shoulders, and went back to the voice of Ilana. Gad doesn't know that I am death, I thought to myself. But John Dawson's mother, sitting near the window of her London flat, must surely know. She is gazing out into the night, and the night has a thousand eyes, which are mine.

"No, Mrs. Dawson, we are not murderers. Your Cabinet ministers are murderers; they are responsible for the death of your son. We should have preferred to receive him as a brother, to offer him bread and milk and show him the beauties of our country. But your government made him our enemy and by the same token signed his death warrant. No, we are not murderers."

I buried my head in my hands. The child outside had stopped crying.

IN ALL PROBABILITY I had killed before, but under entirely different circumstances. The act had other dimensions, other witnesses. Since my arrival in Palestine several months before, I had taken part in various tangles with the police, in sabotage operations, in attacks on military convoys making their way across the green fields of Galilee or the white desert. There had been casualties on both sides, but the odds were in our favor because the night was our ally. Under cover of darkness we took the enemy by surprise; we set fire to an army encampment, killed a dozen soldiers, and disappeared without leaving any traces behind us. The Movement's objective was to kill the greatest number of soldiers possible. It was that simple.

Ever since the day of my arrival, my first steps on the soil of Palestine, this idea had been imprinted upon my brain. As I stepped off the ship at Haifa two comrades picked me up in their car and took me to a two-storey house somewhere between Ramat-Gan and Tel Aviv. This house was ostensibly occupied by a professor of languages, to justify the comings and goings of a large number of young people who were actually, like myself, apprentices of a school of terrorist techniques. The cellar served as a dungeon where we kept prisoners, hostages, and those of our comrades who were wanted by the police. Here it was that John Dawson was awaiting execution. The hiding place was absolutely secure. Several times English soldiers had searched the house from top to bottom; their police dogs had come within a few inches of John Dawson, but there was a wall between them.

Gad directed our terrorist instruction. Other masked teachers taught us the use of a revolver, a machine gun, a hand grenade. We learned also to wield a dagger, to strangle a man from behind without making a sound, and to get out of practically any prison. The course lasted for six weeks. For two hours every day Gad indoctrinated us with the Movement's ideology. The goal was simply to get the English out; the method, intimidation, terror, and sudden death.

"On the day when the English understand that their occupation will cost them blood they won't want to stay," Gad told us. "It's cruel—inhuman, if you like. But we have no other choice. For generations we've wanted to be better, more pure in heart than those who persecuted us. You've all seen the result: Hitler and the extermination camps in Germany. We've had enough of trying to be more just than those who claim to speak in the name of justice. When the Nazis killed a third of our people just men found nothing to say. If ever it's a question of killing off Jews, everyone is silent; there are twenty centuries of history to prove it. We can rely only on ourselves. If we must become more unjust and inhuman than those who have been unjust and inhuman to us, then we shall do so. We don't like to be bearers of death; heretofore we've chosen to be victims rather than executioners. The commandment *Thou shalt not kill* was given from the summit of one of the mountains here in Palestine, and we were the only ones to obey it. But that's all over; we must be like everybody else. Murder will be not our profession but our duty. In the days and weeks and months to come you will have only one purpose: to kill those who have made us killers. We shall kill in order that once more we may be men . . ."

On the last day of the course a masked stranger addressed us. He spoke of what our leaders called the eleventh commandment: *Hate your enemy.* He had a soft, timid, romantic voice, and I think he was the Old Man. I'm not quite sure, but his words fired our enthusiasm and made us tremble with emotion. Long after he had gone away I felt them vibrate within me. Thanks to him I became part of a Messianic world where destiny had the face of a masked beggar, where not a single act was lost or a single glance wasted.

I remembered how the grizzled master had explained the sixth commandment to me. Why has a man no right to commit murder? Because in so doing he takes upon himself the function of God. And this must not be done too easily. Well, I said to myself, if in order to change the course of our history we have to become God, we shall become Him. How easy that is we shall see. No, it was not easy.

The first time I took part in a terrorist operation I had to make a superhuman effort not be sick at my stomach. I found myself utterly hateful. Seeing myself with the eyes of the past I imagined that I was in the dark gray uniform of an SS officer. The first time . . .

THEY RAN LIKE RABBITS, like drunken rabbits, looking for the shelter of a tree. They seemed to have neither heads nor hands, but only legs. And these legs ran like rabbits sotted with wine and sorrow. But we were all around them, forming a circle of fire from which there was no escape. We were there with our tommy guns, and our bullets were a flaming wall on which their lives were shattered to the accompaniment of agonized cries which I shall hear until the last day of my life.

There were six of us. I don't remember the names of the five others, but Gad was not among them. That day he stayed at the school, as if to show that he had complete confidence in us, as if he were saying: "Go to it; you can get along without me." My five comrades and I set out either to kill or to be killed.

"Good luck!" said Gad as he shook hands with us before we went away. "I'll wait here for your return."

This was the first time that I had been assigned to any operation, and I knew that when I came back—if I came back—I should be another man. I should have undergone my baptism of fire, my baptism of blood. I knew that I should feel very differently, but I had no idea that I should be ready to vomit.

Our mission was to attack a military convoy on the road between Haifa and Tel Aviv. The exact spot was the curve near the village of Hedera; the time late afternoon. In the disguise of workmen coming home from their job we arrived at the chosen place thirty minutes before H-hour. If we had come any earlier our presence might have attracted attention. We set mines on either side of the curve and moved into planned positions. A car was waiting fifty yards away to take us to Petach Tivka, where we were to split up and be driven in three other cars back to our base at the school.

The convoy arrived punctually upon the scene: three open trucks carrying about twenty soldiers. The wind ruffled their hair and the sun shone upon their faces. At the curve the first truck was exploded by one of our mines and the others came to an abrupt halt with screeching brakes. The soldiers leaped to the ground and were caught in the cross-fire of our guns. They ran with lowered heads in every direction, but their legs were cut by our bullets, as if by an immense scythe, and they fell shrieking to the ground.

The whole episode lasted no more than a single minute. We withdrew in good order and everything went according to plan. Our mission was accomplished. Gad was waiting at the school and we made our report to him. His face glowed with pride.

"Good work," he said. "The Old Man won't believe it."

It was then that nausea overcame me. I saw the legs running like frightened rabbits and I found myself utterly hateful. I remembered the dreaded SS guards in the Polish ghettos. Day after day, night after night, they slaughtered the Jews in just the same way. Tommy guns were scattered here and there, and an officer, laughing or distractedly eating, barked out the order: *Fire!* Then the scythe went to work. A few Jews tried to break through the circle of fire, but they only rammed their heads against its insurmountable wall. They too ran like rabbits, like rabbits sotted with wine and sorrow, and death mowed them down.

NO, IT WAS NOT EASY to play the part of God, especially when it meant putting on the field-gray uniform of the SS. But it was easier than killing a hostage.

In the first operation and those that followed I was not alone. I killed, to be sure, but I was one of a group. With John Dawson I would be on my own. I would look into his face and he would look into mine and see that I was all eyes.

"Don't torture yourself, Elisha," said Gad. He had turned off the radio and was scrutinizing me intently. "This is war."

I wanted to ask him whether God, the God of war, wore a uniform. But I chose to keep silent. God doesn't wear a uniform, I said to myself. God is a member of the Resistance movement, a terrorist.

ILANA ARRIVED a few minutes before the curfew with her two bodyguards, Gideon and Joab. She was restless and somber, more beautiful than ever. Her delicate features seemed chiseled out of brown marble and there was an expression of heartrending melancholy on her face. She was wearing a gray skirt and a white blouse and her lips were very pale.

"Unforgettable . . . that broadcast of yours," murmured Gad.

"The Old Man wrote it," said Ilana.

"But your voice . . ."

"That's the Old Man's creation, too," said Ilana, sinking exhausted into a chair. And after a moment of complete silence she added: "Today I saw him crying. I have an idea that he cries more often than we know."

The lucky fellow, I thought to myself. At least he can cry. When a man weeps he knows that one day he will stop.

Joab gave us the latest news of Tel Aviv, of its atmosphere of anxiety and watchful waiting. People were afraid of mass reprisals, and all the newspapers had appealed to the Old Man to call off John Dawson's execution. The name of John Dawson rather than that of David ben Moshe was on everyone's lips.

"That's why the Old Man was crying," said Gad, brushing a stubborn lock of hair back from his forehead. "The Jews are not yet free of their persecution reflex. They haven't the guts to strike back."

"In London the Cabinet is in session," Joab went on. "In New York the Zionists are holding a huge demonstration in Madison Square Garden. The UN is deeply concerned."

"I hope David knows," said Ilana. Her face had paled to a bronze hue.

"No doubt the hangman will tell him," said Gad.

I understood the bitterness in his voice. David was a childhood friend and they had entered the Movement together. Gad had told me this only after David's arrest, for it would have been unsafe before. The less any one of us knew about his comrades the better; this is one of the basic principles of any underground organization.

Gad had been present when David was wounded; in fact, he was in command of the operation. It was supposed to be what we called a "soft job," but the courageous stupidity of a sentry had spoiled it. His was the fault if David was to be hanged on the morrow. Although wounded and in convulsions he had continued to crawl along the ground with a bullet in his belly and even to shoot off his gun. The mischief that a courageous, diehard fool can do!

IT WAS NIGHT. An army truck came to a halt at the entrance of the red-capped paratroopers' camp near Gedera, in the south. In it were a major and three soldiers.

"We've come to get some arms," the major said to the sentry. "A terrorist attack is supposed to take place this evening."

"Those goddamned terrorists," the sentry mumbled from under his mustache, handing back the major's identification papers.

"Very good, major," he said, opening the gate. "You can come in."

"Thanks," said the major. "Where are the stores?"

"Straight ahead and then two left turns."

The car drove through, followed these directions and stopped in front of a stone building.

"Here we are," said the major.

They got out, and a sergeant saluted the major and opened the door. The major returned his salute and handed him an order with a colonel's signature at the bottom, an order to consign to the bearer five tommy guns, twenty rifles, twenty revolvers, and the necessary ammunition.

"We're expecting a terrorist attack," the major explained condescendingly.

"Goddamned terrorists," muttered the sergeant.

"We've no time to lose," the major added. "Can you hurry?"

"Of course, sir," said the sergeant. "I quite understand."

He pointed out the arms and ammunition to the three soldiers, who silently and quickly loaded them onto the truck. In a very few minutes it was all done.

"I'll just keep this order, sir," said the sergeant as the visitors started to go away.

"Right you are, Sergeant," said the major, climbing into the truck.

The sentry was just about to open the gate when in his sentry box the telephone rang. With a hasty apology he went to answer. The major and his men waited impatiently.

"Sorry, sir," said the sentry as he emerged from the box. "The sergeant wants to see you. He says the order you brought him is not satisfactory."

The major got down from the truck.

"I'll clear it up with him on the telephone," he said.

As the sentry turned around to re-enter the box the major brought his fist down on the back of his neck. The sentry fell noiselessly to the ground. Gad went over to the gate, opened it, and signaled to the driver to go through. Just then the sentry came to and started shooting. Dan put a bullet into his belly while Gad jumped onto the truck and called out:

"Let's go! And hurry!"

The wounded sentry continued to shoot and one of his bullets punctured a tire. Gad retained his self-possession and decided that the tire must be changed.

"David and Dan, keep us covered," he said in a quiet, assured voice.

David and Dan grabbed two of the recently received tommy guns and stood by.

By now the whole camp was alerted. Orders rang out and gunfire followed. Every second was precious. Covered by David and Dan, Gad changed the tire. But the paratroopers were drawing near. Gad knew that the important thing was to make off with the weapons.

"David and Dan," he said, "stay where you are. We're leaving. See if you can hold them back for three minutes longer while we get away. After that you can make a dash for it. Try to get to Gedera, where friends will give you shelter. You know where to find them."

"Yes, I know," said David, continuing to shoot. "Go on, and hurry!"

The arms and ammunition were saved, but David and Dan had to pay. Dan was killed and David wounded. All on account of a stubbornly courageous sentry with a bullet in his belly!

"HE WAS A WONDERFUL FELLOW, David," said Ilana. Already she spoke of him as if he belonged to the past.

"I hope the hangman knows it," retorted Gad.

I understood his bitterness; indeed I envied it. He was losing a friend, and it hurt. But when you lose a friend every day it doesn't hurt so much. And I'd lost plenty of friends in my time; sometimes I thought of myself as a living graveyard. That was the real reason I followed Gad to Palestine and became a terrorist: I had no more friends to lose.

"They say that the hangman always wears a mask," said Joab, who had been standing silently in front of the kitchen door. "I wonder if it's true."

"I think it is," I said. "The hangman wears a mask. You can't see anything but his eyes."

Ilana went over to Gad, stroked his hair, and said in a sad voice:

"Don't torture yourself, Gad. This is war."

URING THE HOUR that followed nobody said a word. They were all thinking of David ben Moshe. David was not alone in his death cell; his friends were with him. All except me. I did not think of David except when they pronounced his name. When they were silent my thoughts went out to someone else, to a man I did not yet know, any more than I knew David, but whom I was fated to know. My David ben Moshe had the name and face of an Englishman, Captain John Dawson.

We sat around the table and Ilana served us some steaming tea. For some time we sipped it without speaking. We looked into the golden liquid in our cups as if we were searching in it for the next step after our silence and the meaning of the events which had brought it about. Then, in order to kill time, we spoke of our memories, of such of them that centered on death.

"Death saved my life," Joab began.

He had a young, innocent, tormented face; dark, confused eyes, and hair as white as that of an old man. He wore a perpetually sleepy expression and yawned from one end of the day to the other.

"A neighbor who was against us because of his pacifist convictions reported me to the police," he went on. "I took shelter in an insane asylum whose superintendent was an old school friend. I stayed there for two weeks, until the police found my traces. 'Is he here?' they asked the superintendent. 'Yes,' he admitted. 'He's here; he's a very sick man.' 'What's the matter with him?' they asked. 'He imagines he's dead,' the superintendent told them. But they insisted on seeing me. I was brought to the superintendent's office, where two police officials assigned to the antiterrorist campaign were waiting. They spoke to me but I did not answer. They asked me questions but I pretended not to hear. Even so, they were not convinced that I was crazy. Overriding the superintendent's protest, they took me away and submitted me to forty-eight hours of interrogation. I played dead, and played it successfully. I refused to eat or drink; when they slapped my hands and face I did not react. Dead men feel no pain and so they do not cry. After forty-eight hours I was taken back to the asylum."

As I listened to Joab various thoughts floated to the surface of my mind. I remembered hearing some of my comrades refer to Joab as the Madman.

"Funny, isn't it?" he said. "Death actually saved my life."

We kept silence for several minutes, as if to pay homage to death for saving his life and giving the name of Madman to a fellow with an innocent, tormented face.

"Several days later, when I left the asylum, I saw that my hair had turned white," Joab concluded.

"That's one of death's little jokes," I put in. "Death loves to change the color of people's hair. Death has no hair; it has only eyes. God, on the other hand, has no eyes at all."

"God saved me from death," said Gideon.

We called Gideon the Saint. First because he *was* a saint, and second because he looked like one. He was a husky, inarticulate fellow some twenty years old, who took pains to make himself inconspicuous and was always mumbling prayers. He wore a beard and side curls, went nowhere without a prayer book in his pocket. His father was a rabbi, and when he learned that his son meant to become a terrorist he gave him his blessing. There are times, his father said, when words and prayers are not enough. The God of grace is also the God of war. And war is not a matter of mere words.

"God saved me from death," Gideon repeated. "His eyes saved me. I too was arrested and tortured. They pulled my beard, lit matches under my fingernails, and spat in my face, all in order to make me confess that I had taken part in an attempt against the life of the High Commissioner. But in spite of the pain I did not talk. More than once I was tempted to cry out, but I kept quiet because I felt that God's eyes were upon me. God is looking at me, I said to myself, and I must not disappoint Him. My torturers never stopped shouting, but I kept my thoughts on God and on His eyes, which are drawn to human pain. For lack of evidence they finally had to set me free. If I had admitted my guilt I should be dead."

"And then," I put in, "God would have closed His eyes."

Ilana refilled our cups.

"What about you, Ilana?" I asked. "What saved your life?"

"A cold in the head," she replied.

I burst out laughing, but no one else joined in. My laugh was raucous and artificial.

"A cold in the head?" I repeated.

"Yes," said Ilana, quite seriously. "The English have no description of me; they know only my voice. One day they hauled in a whole group of women, myself among them. At the police station a sound engineer compared each one of our voices to that of the mysterious announcer of the Voice of Freedom. Thanks to the fact that I had a heavy cold I was quickly eliminated and four other women were detained for further questioning."

Once more I was tempted to laugh, but the others were glum and silent. A cold, I thought to myself. And in this case it turned out to have more practical use than either faith or courage. Next we all looked at Gad, who was almost crushing his teacup between his fingers.

"I owe my life to three Englishmen," he said. With his head almost on his right shoulder and his eyes fixed on the cup, he seemed to be addressing the rapidly cooling tea. "It was very early in the game," he went on. "For reasons that no longer matter the Old Man had ordered three hostages taken. They were all sergeants, and I was assigned to kill one of them, any one; the choice was up to me. I was young then, about the age of Elisha, and suffered great mental agony from having this unwanted role thrust upon me. I was willing to play the executioner, but not the judge. Unfortunately, during the night I lost contact with the Old Man and could not explain my reluctance. The sentence had to be carried out at dawn, and how was I to choose the victim? Finally I had an idea. I went down to the cellar and told the three sergeants that the choice was up to them. If you don't make it, I said, then all three of you will be shot. They decided to draw lots, and when dawn came I put a bullet in the unlucky fellow's neck."

Involuntarily I looked at Gad's hands and face, the familiar hands and face of my friend, who had put a bullet in the neck of a fellow human being and now talked coldly, almost indifferently, about it. Was the sergeant's face gazing up at him from his cup of golden cool tea?

"What if the sergeants had refused to settle it among themselves?" I asked. "What then?"

Gad squeezed the cup harder than ever, almost as if he were trying to break it.

"I think I'd have killed myself instead," he said in a flat voice. And after a moment of heavy silence he added: "I tell you I was young and very weak."

All eyes turned toward me, in expectation of my story. I gulped down a mouthful of bitter tea and wiped the perspiration off my forehead.

"I owe my life to a laugh," I said. "It was during one winter at Buchenwald. We were clothed in rags and hundreds of people died of cold every day. In the morning we had to leave our barracks and wait outside in the snow for as long as two hours until they had been cleaned. One day I felt so sick that I was sure the exposure would kill me, and so I stayed behind, in hiding. Quite naturally I was discovered and the cleaning squad dragged me before one of the many assistant barracks leaders. Without stopping to question me he caught hold of my throat and said dispassionately: 'I'm going to choke you.' His powerful hands closed in on my throat and in my enfeebled condition I did not even try to put up a fight. Very well, I said to myself; it's all over. I felt the blood gather in my head and my head swell to several times its normal size, so that I must have looked like a caricature, a miserable clown. I was sure from one minute to the next that it would burst into a thousand shreds like a child's toy balloon. At this moment the assistant leader took a good look at me and found the sight so comical that he released his grip and burst out laughing. He laughed so long that he forgot his intention to kill. And that's how I got out of it unharmed. It's funny, isn't it, that I should owe my life to an assassin's sense of humor?"

I expected my listeners to scrutinize my head to see if it had really returned to its normal size, but they did nothing of the sort. They continued to stare into their stone-cold tea. In the next few minutes nobody opened his mouth. We had no more desire to call up the past or to listen to our fellows tell their troubled life stories. We sat in restless silence around the table. Every one of us, I am sure, was asking himself to what he *really* owed his life. Gideon was the first to speak.

"We ought to take the Englishman something to eat," he said.

Yes, I said to myself, Gideon is sad, too. He's thinking of John Dawson. He must be; it's inevitable.

"I don't imagine he's hungry," I said aloud. "You can't expect a man condemned to die to have an appetite." And to myself I added: "Or a man condemned to kill, either."

There must have been a strange tone in my voice, for the others raised their heads and I felt the puzzled quality of their penetrating stares.

"No," I said stubbornly; "a man condemned to die can't be hungry."

They did not stir, but sat petrified as the seconds dragged interminably by.

"The condemned man's traditional last meal is a joke," I said loudly, "a joke in the worst possible taste, an insult to the corpse that he is about to be. What does a man care if he dies with an empty stomach?"

The expression of astonishment lingered in Gad's eyes, but Ilana looked at me with compassion and Gideon with friendliness. Joab did not look at me at all. His eyes were lowered, but perhaps that was his way of looking out of them.

"He doesn't know," remarked Gideon.

"He doesn't know what?" I asked, without any conscious reason for raising my voice. Perhaps I wanted to hear myself shout, to arouse my anger and see it reflected in the motionless shadows in the mirror and on the wall. Or perhaps out of sheer weakness. I felt powerless to change anything, least of all myself, in spite of the fact that I wanted to introduce a transformation into the room, to reorder the whole of creation. I would have made the Saint into a madman, have given John Dawson's name to Gad and his fate to David. But I knew there was nothing I could do. To have such power I should have had to take the place of death, not just of the individual death of John Dawson, the English captain who had no more appetite than I.

"What doesn't he know?" I repeated stridently.

"He doesn't know he's going to die," said Gideon in a sorrow-fully dreamy voice.

"His stomach knows," I retorted. "A man about to die listens only to his stomach. He pays no attention to his heart or to his past, or to yours for that matter. He doesn't even hear the voice of the storm. He listens to his stomach and his stomach tells him that he is going to die and that he isn't hungry."

I had talked too fast and too loud and I was left panting. I should have liked to run away, but my friends' stares transfixed me. Death sealed off every exit, and everywhere there were eyes.

"I'm going down to the cellar," said Gideon. "I'll ask him if he wants something to eat."

"Don't ask him anything," I said. "Simply tell him that tomor-row, when the sun rises above the blood-red horizon, he, John Dawson, will say good-by to life, good-by to his stomach. Tell him that he's going to die."

Gideon got up, with his eyes still on me, and started toward the kitchen and the entrance to the cellar. At the door he paused.

"I'll tell him," he said, with a quickly fading smile. Then he turned on his heels and I heard him going down the stairs.

I was grateful for his consent. He and not I would warn John

Dawson of his approaching end. I could never have done it. It's easier to kill a man than to break the news that he is going to die.

"Midnight," said Joab.

Midnight, I reflected, the hour when the dead rise out of their graves and come to say their prayers in the synagogue, the hour when God Himself weeps over the destruction of the Temple, the hour when a man should be able to plumb the depths of his being and to discover the Temple in ruins. A God that weeps and dead men that pray.

"Poor boy!" murmured Ilana.

She did not look at me, but her tears scrutinized my face. Her tears rather than her eyes caressed me.

"Don't say that, Ilana. Don't call me 'poor boy.' "

There were tears in her eyes, or rather there were tears in the place of her eyes, tears which with every passing second grew heavier and more opaque and threatened to overflow . . . I was afraid that suddenly the worst would happen: the dusky Ilana would no longer be there; she would have drowned in her tears. I wanted to touch her arm and say *Don't cry*. Say what you like, but don't cry.

But she wasn't crying. It takes eyes to cry, and she had no eyes, only tears where her eyes should have been.

"Poor boy!" she repeated.

Then what I had foreseen came true. Ilana disappeared, and Catherine was there instead. I wondered why Catherine had come, but her apparition did not particularly surprise me. She liked the opposite sex, and particularly she liked little boys who were thinking of death. She liked to speak of love to little boys, and since men going to their death are little boys she liked to speak to them of love. For this reason her presence in the magical room—magical because it transcended the differences, the boundary lines between the victim and the executioner, between the present and the past—was not surprising.

I had met Catherine in Paris in 1945, when I had just come from Buchenwald, that other magical spot, where the living were transformed into dead and their future into darkness. I was weakened and half starved. One of the many rescue committees sent me to a camp where a hundred boys and girls were spending their summer vacation. The camp was in Normandy, where the early morning breeze rustled the same way it did in Palestine.

Because I knew no French I could not communicate with the other boys and girls. I ate and sunbathed with them, but I had no way of talking. Catherine was the only person who seemed to know any German and occasionally we exchanged a few words. Sometimes she came up to me at the dining-room table and asked me whether I had slept well, enjoyed my meal, or had a good time during the day.

She was twenty-six or -seven years old; small, frail, and almost transparent, with silky blonde, sunlit hair and blue, dreamy eyes which never cried. Her face was thin but saved from being bony by the delicacy of the features. She was the first woman I had seen from nearby. Before this—that is, before the war—I did not look at women. On my way to school or the synagogue I walked close to the walls, with my eyes cast down on the ground. I knew that women existed, and why, but I did not appreciate the fact that they had a body, breasts, legs, hands, and lips whose touch sets a man's heart to beating. Catherine revealed this to me.

The camp was at the edge of a wood, and after supper I went walking there all by myself, talking to the murmuring breeze and watching the sky turn a deeper and deeper blue. I liked to be alone.

One evening Catherine asked if she might go with me, and I

was too timid to say anything but yes. For half an hour, an hour, we walked in complete silence. At first I found the silence embarrassing, then to my surprise I began to enjoy it. The silence of two people is deeper than the silence of one. Involuntarily I began to talk.

"Look how the sky is opening up," I said.

She threw back her head and looked above her. Just as I had said, the sky was opening up. Slowly at first, as if swept by an invisible wind, the stars drew away from the zenith, some moving to the right, others to the left, until the center of the sky was an empty space, dazzlingly blue and gradually acquiring depth and outline.

"Look hard," I said. "There's nothing there."

From behind me Catherine looked up and said not a word.

"That's enough," I said; "let's go on walking."

As we walked on I told her the legend of the open sky. When I was a child the old master told me that there were nights when the sky opened up in order to make way for the prayers of unhappy children. On one such night a little boy whose father was dying said to God: "Father, I am too small to know how to pray. But I ask you to heal my sick father." God did what the boy asked, but the boy himself was turned into a prayer and carried up into Heaven. From that day on, the master told me, God has from time to time shown Himself to us in the face of a child.

"That is why I like to look at the sky at this particular moment," I told Catherine. "I hope to see the child. But you are a witness to the truth. There's nothing there. The child is only a story."

It was then for the first time during the evening that Catherine spoke.

"Poor boy!" she exclaimed. "Poor boy!"

She's thinking of the boy in the story, I said to myself. And I loved her for her compassion.

After this Catherine often went walking with me. She questioned me about my childhood and my more recent past, but I did not always answer. One evening she asked me why I kept apart from the other boys and girls in the camp.

"Because they speak a language I can't understand," I told her.

"Some of the girls know German," she said.

"But I have nothing to say to them."

"You don't have to say anything," she said slowly, with a smile. "All you have to do is love them."

I didn't see what she was driving at and said so. Her smile widened and she began to speak to me of love. She spoke easily and well. Love is this and love is that; man is born to love; he is only alive when he is in the presence of a woman he loves or should love. I told her that I knew nothing of love, that I didn't know it existed or had a right to exist.

"I'll prove it to you," she said.

The next evening, as she walked at my left side over the leaf-covered path, she took hold of my arm. At first I thought she needed my support, but actually it was because she wanted to make me feel the warmth of her body. Then she claimed to be tired and said it would be pleasant to sit down on the grass under a tree. Once we had sat down she began to stroke my face and hair. Then she kissed me several times; first her lips touched mine and then her tongue burned the inside of my mouth. For several nights running we returned to the same place, and she spoke to me of love and desire and the mysteries of the heart. She took my hand and guided it over her breasts and thighs, and I realized that women had breasts and thighs and hands that could set a man's heart to beating and turn his blood to fire.

Then came the last evening. The month of vacation was over and I was to go back to Paris the next day. As soon as we had finished supper we went to sit for the last time under the tree. I felt sad and lonely, and Catherine held my hand in hers without speaking. The night was fair and calm. At intervals, like a warm breath, the wind played over our faces. It must have been one or two o'clock in the morning when Catherine broke the silence, turned her melancholy face toward me, and said:

"Now we're going to make love."

These words made me tremble. I was going to make love for the first time. Before her there had been no woman upon earth. I didn't know what to say or do; I was afraid of saying the wrong thing or making some inappropriate gesture. Awkwardly I waited for her to take the initiative. With a suddenly serious look on her face she began to get undressed. She took off her blouse and in the starlight I saw her ivory-white breasts. Then she took off the rest of her clothes and was completely naked before me.

"Take off your shirt," she ordered.

I was paralyzed; there was iron in my throat and lead in my veins; my arms and hands would not obey me. I could only look at her from head to foot and follow the rise and fall of her breasts. I was hypnotized by the call of her outstretched, naked body.

"Take off your shirt," she repeated.

Then, as I did not move, she began to undress me. Deliberately she took off my shirt and shorts. Then she lay back on the grass and said:

"Take me."

I got down on my knees. I stared at her for a long time and then I covered her body with kisses. Absently and without saying a word she stroked my hair.

"Catherine," I said, "first there is something I must tell you."

Her face took on a blank and anguished expression, and there was anguish in the rustle of the breeze among the trees.

"No, no!" she cried. "Don't tell me anything. Take me, but don't talk."

Heedless of her objection I went on:

"First, Catherine, I must tell you . . ."

Her lips twisted with pain, and there was pain in the rustle of the breeze.

"No, no, no!" she implored. "Don't tell me. Be quiet. Take me quickly, but don't talk."

"What I have to tell you is this," I insisted: "You've won the game. I love you, Catherine . . . I love you."

She burst into sobs and repeated over and over again:

"Poor boy! You poor boy!"

I picked up my shirt and shorts and ran away. Now I understood. She was referring not to the little boy in the sky but to me. She had spoken to me of love because she knew that I was the little boy who had been turned into a prayer and carried up into Heaven. She knew that I had died and come back to earth, dead. This was why she had spoken to me of love and wanted to make love with me. I saw it all quite clearly. She liked making love with little boys who were going to die; she enjoyed the company of those who were obsessed with death. No wonder that her presence this night in Palestine was not surprising.

"Poor boy!" said Ilana, in a very quiet voice, for the last time. And a deep sigh escaped from her breast, which made her tears free to flow, to flow on and on until the end of time.

S UDDENLY I became aware that the room was stuffy, so stuffy that I was almost stifled.

No wonder. The room was small, far too small to receive so many visitors at one time. Ever since midnight the visitors had been pouring in. Among them were people I had known, people I had hated, admired, forgotten. As I let my eyes wander about the room I realized that all of those who had contributed to my formation, to the formation of my permanent identity, were there. Some of them were familiar, but I could not pin a label upon them; they were names without faces or faces without names. And yet I knew that at some point my life had crossed theirs.

My father was there, of course, and my mother, and the beggar. And the grizzled master. The English soldiers of the convoy we had ambushed at Gedera were there also. And around them friends and brothers and comrades, some of them out of my childhood, others that I had seen live and suffer, hope and curse at Buchenwald and Auschwitz. Alongside my father there was a boy who looked strangely like myself as I had been before the concentration camps, before the war, before everything. My father smiled at him, and the child picked up the smile and sent it to me over the multitude of heads which separated us.

Now I understood why the room was so stuffy. It was too small to hold so many people at a time. I forced a passage through the crowd until I came to the little boy and thanked him for the smile. I wanted to ask him what all these people were doing in the room, but on second thought I saw that this would be discourteous toward my father. Since he was present I should address my question to him.

"Father, why are all these people here?"

My mother stood beside him, looking very pale, and her lips tirelessly murmured: "Poor little boy, poor little boy! . . ."

"Father," I repeated, "answer me. What are you all doing here?"

His large eyes, in which I had so often seen the sky open up, were looking at me, but he did not reply. I turned around and found myself face to face with the rabbi, whose beard was more grizzled than ever.

"Master," I said, "what has brought all these people here tonight?"

Behind me I heard my mother whisper, "Poor little boy, my poor little boy."

"Well, Master," I repeated, "answer me, I implore you."

But he did not answer either; indeed, he seemed not even to have heard my question, and his silence made me afraid. As I had known him before, he was always present in my hour of need. Then his silence had been reassuring. Now I tried to look into his eyes, but they were two globes of fire, two suns that burned my face. I turned away and went from one visitor to another, seeking an answer to my question, but my presence struck them dumb.

Finally I came to the beggar, who stood head and shoulders above them all. And he spoke to me, quite spontaneously.

"This is a night of many faces," he said.

I was sad and tired.

"Yes," I said wearily, "this is a night of many faces, and I should like to know the reason why. If you are the one I think you are, enlighten and comfort me. Tell me the meaning of these looks, this muteness, these presences. Tell me, I beseech you, for I can endure them no longer."

He took my arm, gently pressed it, and said:

"Do you see that little boy over there?" and he pointed to the boy who looked like myself as I had been.

"Yes, I see him," I replied.

"He will answer all your questions," said the beggar. "Go talk to him."

Now I was quite sure that he was not a beggar. Once more I elbowed my way through the crowd of ghosts and arrived, panting with exhaustion, at the young boy's side.

"Tell me," I said beseechingly, "what you are doing here? And all the others?"

He opened his eyes wide in astonishment.

"Don't you know?" he asked.

I confessed that I did not know.

"Tomorrow a man is to die, isn't he?"

"Yes," I said, "at dawn tomorrow."

"And you are to kill him, aren't you?"

"Yes, that's true; I have been charged with his execution."

"And you don't understand, do you?"

"No."

"But it's all quite simple," he exclaimed. "We are here to be present at the execution. We want to see you carry it out. We want to see you turn into a murderer. That's natural enough, isn't it?"

"How is it natural? Of what concern is the killing of John Dawson to you?"

"You are the sum total of all that we have been," said the youngster who looked like my former self. "In a way we are the ones to execute John Dawson. Because you can't do it without us. Now, do you see?"

I was beginning to understand. An act so absolute as that of killing involves not only the killer but, as well, those who have formed him. In murdering a man I was making them murderers.

"Well," said the boy, "do you see?"

"Yes, I see," I said.

"Poor boy, poor boy!" murmured my mother, whose lips were now as gray as the old master's hair.

"HE'S HUNGRY," said Gideon's voice, unexpectedly.

I had not heard him come back up the stairs. Saints have a disconcertingly noiseless way. They walk, laugh, eat, and pray, all without making a sound.

"Impossible," I protested.

He can't be hungry, I was thinking. He's going to die, and a man who's going to die can't be hungry.

"He said so himself," Gideon insisted, with a shade of emotion in his voice.

Everyone was staring at me. Ilana had stopped crying, Joab was no longer examining his nails, and Gad looked weary. All the ghosts, too, seemed to be expecting something of me, a sign perhaps, or a cry.

"Does he know?" I asked Gideon.

"Yes, he knows." And after a moment he added: "I told him."

"How did he react?"

It was important for me to know the man's reaction. Was the

news a shock? Had he stayed calm, or protested his innocence?

"He smiled," said Gideon. "He said that he already knew. His stomach had told him."

"And he said he was hungry?"

Gideon hid his twitching hands behind his back.

"Yes, that's what he said. He said he was hungry and he had a right to a good last meal."

Gad laughed, but the tone of his laugh was hollow.

"Typically English," he remarked. "The stiff upper lip."

His remark hung over our heads in midair; no one opened up to receive it. My father shot me a hard glance, as if to say *A man is going to die, and he's hungry.*

"Might as well admit it," said Gad. "The English have iron digestions."

No one paid any attention to this remark either. I felt a sudden stab of pain in my stomach. I had not eaten all day. Ilana got up and went into the kitchen.

"I'll fix him something to eat," she declared.

I heard her moving about, slicing a loaf of bread, opening the icebox, starting to make coffee. In a few minutes she came back with a cup of coffee in one hand and a plate in the other.

"This is all I can find," she said. "A cheese sandwich and some black coffee. There's no sugar . . . Not much of a meal, but it's the best I can do." And after several seconds of silence she asked: "Who's going to take it down?"

The boy standing beside my father stared hard at me. His stare had a voice, which said:

"Go on. Take him something to eat. He's hungry, you know."

"No," I responded. "Not I. I don't want to see him. Above all, I don't want to see him eat. I want to think of him, later on, as a man who never ate."

I wanted to add that I had cramps in my stomach, but I realized that this was unimportant. Instead I said: "I don't want to be alone with him. Not now."

"We'll go with you," said the little boy. "It's wrong to hold back food from a man who's hungry. You know that."

Yes, I knew. I had always given food to the hungry. You, beggar, you remember. Didn't I offer you bread? But tonight is different. Tonight I can't do it.

"That's true," said the little boy, picking up the train of my reflections. "Tonight is different, and you are different also, or at least you're going to be. But that has nothing to do with the fact that a man's hungry and must have something to eat."

"But he's going to die tomorrow," I protested. "What's it matter whether he dies with a full stomach or an empty one?"

"For the time being he's alive," the child said sententiously. My father nodded in acquiescence, and all the others followed his example. "He's alive and hungry, and you refuse to give him anything to eat?"

All these heads, nodding like the tops of black trees, made me shudder. I wanted to close my eyes but I was ashamed. I couldn't close my eyes in the presence of my father.

"Very well," I said resignedly. "I accept. I'll take him something to eat." As if obeying the baton of an invisible conductor the nodding heads were still. "I'll take him something to eat," I repeated. "But first tell me something, little boy. Are the dead hungry too?"

He looked surprised.

"What—you don't know?" he exclaimed. "Of course they are."

"And should we give them something to eat?"

"How can you ask? Of course you should give them something to eat. Only it's difficult . . ."

"Difficult . . . difficult . . . difficult . . . ," the ghosts echoed together.

The boy looked at me and smiled.

"I'll tell you a secret," he whispered. "You know that at midnight the dead leave their graves, don't you?"

I told him that I knew; I had been told.

"Have you been told that they go from the graveyard to the synagogue?"

Yes, I had been told that also.

"Well, it's true," said the little boy. Then, after a silence which accentuated what was to follow, he went on in a voice so still that if it had not been inside myself I could never have heard it: "Yes, it's true. They gather every night in the synagogue. But not for the purpose you imagine. They come not to pray but to eat—"

Everything in the room—walls, chairs, heads—began to whirl around me, dancing in a pre-established rhythm, without stirring the air or setting foot on the ground. I was the center of a multitude of circles. I wanted to close my eyes and stop up my ears, but my father was there, and my mother, and the master and the beggar and the boy. With all those who had formed me around me I had no right to stop up my ears and close my eyes.

"Give me those things," I said to Ilana. "I'll take them to him."

The dancers stopped in their tracks, as if I were the conductor and my words his baton. I stepped toward Ilana, still standing at the kitchen door. Suddenly Gad rushed forward and reached her side before me.

"I'll do it," he said.

Almost brutally he snatched the cup and plate from Ilana's hands and went precipitately down the stairs.

Joab looked at his watch. "It's after two."

"Is that all?" asked Ilana. "It's a long night, the longest I've ever lived through."

"Yes, it's long," Joab agreed.

Ilana bit her lips. "There are moments when I think it will never end, that it will last indefinitely. It's like the rain. Here the rain, like everything else, suggests permanence and eternity. I say to myself: It's raining today and it's going to rain tomorrow and the next day, the next week and the next century. Now I say to myself: There's night now and there will be night tomorrow, and the day, the week, the century after."

She paused abruptly, took a handkerchief from the cuff of her blouse and wiped her perspiring forehead.

"I wonder why it's so stuffy in here," she said, "particularly this late at night."

"It will be cooler early tomorrow," promised Joab.

"I hope so," said Ilana. "What time does the sun rise?"

"Around five o'clock."

"And what time is it now?"

"Twenty past two," said Joab, looking again at his watch.

"Aren't you hot, Elisha?" Ilana asked me.

"Yes, I am," I answered.

Ilana went back to her place at the table. I walked over to the window and looked out. The city seemed faraway and unreal. Deep in sleep, it spawned anxious dreams, hopeful dreams, dreams which would proliferate other dreams on the morrow. And these dreams in their turn would engender new heroes, who would live through the night and prepare to die at dawn, to die and to give death.

"Yes, I'm hot, Ilana," I said. "I'm stifling."

I DON'T KNOW how long I stood, sweating, beside the open window, before a warm, vibrant, reassuring hand was laid on my shoulder. It was Ilana.

"What are you thinking?" she said.

"I'm thinking of the night," I told her. "Always the same thing—"

"And of John Dawson?"

"Yes, of John Dawson."

Somewhere in the city a light shone in a window and then went out. No doubt a man had looked at his watch or a mother had gone to find out whether her child was smiling in his sleep.

"You didn't want to see him, though," said Ilana.

"I don't want to see him."

One day, I was thinking, my son will say: "All of a sudden you look sad. What's wrong?" "It's because in my eyes there is a picture of an English captain called John Dawson, just as he appeared to me at the moment of his death . . ." Perhaps I ought to put a mask on his face; a mask is more easily killed and forgotten.

"Are you afraid?" asked Ilana.

"Yes."

Being afraid, I ought to have told her, is nothing. Fear is only a color, a backdrop, a landscape. That isn't the problem. The fear of either the victim or the executioner is unimportant. What matters is the fact that each of them is playing a role which has been imposed upon him. The two roles are the extremities of the estate of man. The tragic thing is the imposition.

"You, Elisha, *you* are afraid?"

I knew why she had asked. You, Elisha, who lived through Auschwitz and Buchenwald? You who any number of times saw God die? You are afraid?

"I *am* afraid, though, Ilana," I repeated.

She knew quite well that fear was not in fact the real theme. Like death, it is only a backdrop, a bit of local color.

"What makes you afraid?"

Her warm, living hand was still on my shoulder; her breasts brushed me and I could feel her breath on my neck. Her blouse was wet with perspiration and her face distraught. She doesn't understand, I thought to myself.

"I'm afraid he'll make me laugh," I said. "You see, Ilana, he's quite capable of swelling up his head and letting it burst into a thousand shreds, just in order to make me laugh. That's what makes me afraid."

But still she did not understand. She took the handkerchief from her cuff and wiped my neck and temples. Then she kissed my forehead lightly and said:

"You torture yourself too much, Elisha. Hostages aren't clowns. There's nothing so funny about them."

Poor Ilana! Her voice was as pure as truth, as sad as purity. But she did not understand. She was distracted by the externals and did not see what lay behind them.

"You may be right," I said in resignation. "We make *them* laugh. They laugh when they're dead."

She stroked my face and neck and hair, and I could still feel the pressure of her breasts against my body. Then she began to talk, in a sad but clear voice, as if she were talking to a sick child.

"You torture yourself too much, my dear," she said several times in succession. At least she no longer called me "poor boy," and I was grateful. "You mustn't do it. You're young and intelligent, and you've suffered quite enough already. Soon it will all be over. The English will get out and we shall come back to the surface and lead a simple, normal life. You'll get married and have children. You'll tell them stories and make them laugh. You'll be happy because they're happy, and they *will* be happy, I promise you. How could they be otherwise with a father like you? You'll have forgotten this night, this room, me, and everything else—"

As she said "everything else" she traced a sweeping semicircle with her hand. I was reminded of my mother. She talked in the same moving voice and used almost the same words in the same places. I was very fond of my mother. Every evening, until I was nine or ten years old, she put me to sleep with lullabies or stories. There is a goat beside your bed, she used to tell me, a goat of gold. Everywhere you go in life the goat will guide and protect you. Even when you are grown up and very rich, when you know everything a man can know and possess all that he should possess, the goat will still be near you.

"You talk as if you were my mother, Ilana," I said.

My mother, too, had a harmonious voice, even more harmonious than Ilana's. Like the voice of God it had power to dispel chaos and to impart a vision of the future which might have been mine, with the goat to guide me, the goat I had lost on the way to Buchenwald.

"You're suffering," said Ilana. "That's what it means when a man speaks of his mother."

"No, Ilana," I said. "At this moment she's the one to suffer."

Ilana's caresses became lighter, more remote. She was beginning to understand. A shadow fell across her face. For some time she was silent, then she joined me in looking at the hand night held out to us through the window.

"War is like night," she said. "It covers everything."

Yes, she was beginning to understand. I hardly felt the pressure of her fingers on my neck.

"We say that ours is a holy war," she went on, "that we're struggling against something and for something, against the English and for an independent Palestine. That's what we say. But these are words; as such they serve only to give meaning to our actions. And our actions, seen in their true and primitive light, have the odor and color of blood. This is war, we say; we must kill. There are those, like you, who kill with their hands, and others—like me—who kill with their voices. Each to his own. And what else can we do? War has a code, and if you deny this you deny its whole purpose and hand the enemy victory on a silver platter. That we can't afford. We need victory, victory in war, in order to survive, in order to remain afloat on the surface of time."

She did not raise her voice. It seemed as if she were chanting a lullaby, telling a bedtime story. There was neither passion nor despair nor even concern in her intonation.

All things considered, she was quite right. We were at war; we had an ideal, a purpose—and also an enemy who stood between us and its attainment. The enemy must be eliminated. And how? By any and all means at our command. There were all sorts of means, but they were unimportant and soon forgotten. The purpose, the end, this was all that would last. Ilana was probably correct in saying that one day I should forget this night. But the dead never forget; they would remember. In their eyes I should be forever branded a killer. There are not a thousand ways of being a killer; either a man is one or he isn't. He can't say I'll kill only ten or only twenty-six men; I'll kill for only five minutes or a single day. He who has killed one man alone is a killer for life. He may choose another occupation, hide himself under another identity, but the executioner or at least the executioner's mask will be always with him. There lies the problem: in the influence of the backdrop of the play upon the actor. War had made me an executioner, and an executioner I would remain even after the backdrop had changed, when I was acting in another play upon a different stage.

"I don't want to be a killer," I said, sliding rapidly over the word as I ejected it.

"Who does?" said Ilana.

She was still stroking my neck, but somehow I had the impression that it was not really *my* neck, *my* hair her fingers were caressing. The noblest woman in the world would hesitate to touch the skin of a killer, of a man who would have the label of killer his whole life long.

I cast a rapid glance behind me to see if the others were still there. Gideon and Joab were dozing, with their heads pillowed on their arms, on the table. Gideon seemed, even in his sleep, to be praying. Gad was still in the cellar and I wondered why he had stayed there so long. As for the ghosts, they followed the conversation but, to my surprise, took no part in it. Ilana was silent.

"What are you thinking?" I murmured.

She did not reply and after a few minutes I posed the question again. Still there was no answer. We were both silent. And the crowd behind me, the crowd of petrified silences, whose shadows absorbed the light and turned it into something sad, funereal, hostile, was silent as well. The sum of these silences filled me with fear. Their silences were different from mine; they were hard, cold, immobile, lifeless, incapable of change.

As a child I had been afraid of the dead and of the graveyard, their shadowy kingdom. The silence with which they surrounded themselves provoked my terror. I knew that now, at my back, in serried ranks as if to protect themselves from the cold, they were sitting in judgment upon me. In their frozen world the dead have nothing to do but judge, and because they have no sense of past or future they judge without pity. They condemn not with words or gestures but with their very existence.

At my back they were sitting in judgment upon me; I felt their silences judging mine. I wanted to turn around but the mere idea filled me with fear. Soon Gad will come up from the cellar, I said to myself, and later it will be my turn to go down. Dawn will come, and this crowd will melt into the light of day. For the present I shall stay beside Ilana, at the window, with my back to them.

A minute later I changed my mind. My father and mother, the master and the beggar were all there. I could not insult them indefinitely by turning my back; I must look at them face to face. Cautiously I wheeled around. There were two sorts of light in the room: one white, around the sleeping Gideon and Joab, the other black, enveloping the ghosts.

I left Ilana lost in thought, perhaps in regret, at the window, and began to walk about the room, pausing every now and then before a familiar face, a familiar sorrow. I knew that these faces, these sorrows, were sitting in judgment upon me. They were dead and they were hungry. When the dead are hungry they judge the living without pity. They do not wait until an action has been achieved, a crime committed. They judge in advance.

Only when I perceived the silence of the boy, a silence eloquent in his eyes, did I decide to speak. He had a look of anxiety which made him seem older, more mature. I shall speak up, I said to myself. They have no right to condemn the little boy.

As I approached my father I saw the sorrow on his face. My father had stolen away a minute before the Angel of Death came to take him; in cheating the Angel he had taken with him the human sorrow which he endured while he was alive.

"Father," I said, "don't judge me. Judge God. He created the universe and made justice stem from injustices. He brought it about that a people should attain happiness through tears, that the freedom of a nation, like that of a man, should be a monument built upon a pile, a foundation of dead bodies . . ."

I stood in front of him, not knowing what to do with my head, my eyes, my hands. I wanted to transfer the lifeblood of my body into my voice. At moments I fancied I had done so. I talked for a long time, telling him things that doubtless he already knew, since he had taught them to me. If I repeated them it was only in order to prove to him that I had not forgotten.

"Don't judge me, Father," I implored him, trembling with despair. "You must judge God. He is the first cause, the prime mover; He conceived men and things the way they are. You are dead, father, and only the dead may judge God."

But he did not react. The sorrow written upon his emaciated, unshaven face became even more human than before. I left him and went over to my mother, who was standing at his right side. But my pain was too great for me to address her. I thought I heard her murmur: "Poor boy, poor boy!" and tears came to my eyes. Finally I said that I wasn't a murderer, that she had not given birth to a murderer but to a soldier, to a fighter for freedom, to an idealist who had sacrificed his peace of mind—a possession more precious than life itself—to his people, to his people's right to the light of day, to joy, to the laughter of children. In a halting, feverishly sobbing voice, this was all that I could find to say.

When she too failed to react I left her and went to my old master, of all those present the least changed by death. Alive, he had been very much the same as now; we used to say that he was not of this world, and now this was literally true.

"I haven't betrayed you," I said, as if the deed were already done. "If I were to refuse to obey orders I should betray my living friends. And the living have more rights over us than the dead. You told me that yourself. *Therefore choose life*, it is written in the Scriptures. I have espoused the cause of the living, and that is no betrayal."

Beside him stood Yerachmiel, my friend and comrade and brother. Yerachmiel was the son of a coachman, with the hands of a laborer and the soul of a saint. We two were the master's favorite pupils; every evening he studied with us the secrets of the Cabala. I did not know that Yerachmiel too was dead. I realized it only at the moment when I saw him in the crowd, at the master's side—or rather a respectful step behind him.

"Yerachmiel my brother," I said, ". . . remember . . . ?"

Together we had spun impossible dreams. According to the

Cabala, if a man's soul is sufficiently pure and his love deep enough he can bring the Messiah to earth. Yerachmiel and I decided to try. Of course we were aware of the danger: No one can force God's hand with impunity. Men older, wiser, and more mature than ourselves had tried in vain to wrest the Messiah from the chains of the future; failing in their purpose they had lost their faith, their reason, and even their lives. Yerachmiel and I knew all this, but we were resolved to carry out our plan regardless of the obstacles that lay in wait along the way. We promised to stick to each other, whatever might happen. If one of us were to die, the other would carry on. And so we made preparations for a voyage in depth. We purified our souls and bodies, fasting by day and praying by night. In order to cleanse our mouths and their utterances we spoke as little as possible and on the Sabbath we spoke not at all.

Perhaps our attempt might have been successful. But war broke out and we were driven away from our homes. The last time I had seen Yerachmiel he was one of a long column of marching Jews deported to Germany. A week later I was sent to Germany myself. Yerachmiel was in one camp, I in another. Often I wondered whether he had continued his efforts alone. Now I knew: he had continued, and he was dead.

"Yerachmiel," I said; "Yerachmiel my brother, remember . . ."

Something about him had changed: his hands. Now they were the hands of a saint.

"We too," I said, "my comrades in the Movement and I, are trying to force God's hand. You who are dead should help us, not hinder . . ."

But Yerachmiel and his hands were silent. And somewhere in the universe of time the Messiah was silent as well. I left him and went over to the little boy I used to be.

"Are you too judging me?" I asked. "You of all people have

the least right to do that. You're lucky; you died young. If you'd gone on living you'd be in my place."

Then the boy spoke. His voice was filled with echoes of disquiet and longing.

"I'm not judging you," he said. "We're not here to sit in judgment. We're here simply because you're here. We're present wherever you go; we are what you do. When you raise your eyes to Heaven we share in their sight; when you pat the head of a hungry child a thousand hands are laid on his head; when you give bread to a beggar we give him that taste of paradise which only the poor can savor. Why are we silent? Because silence is not only our dwelling-place but our very being as well. We *are* silence. And your silence is us. You carry us with you. Occasionally you may see us, but most of the time we are invisible to you. When you see us you imagine that we are sitting in judgment upon you. You are wrong. Your silence is your judge."

Suddenly the beggar's arm brushed against mine. I turned and saw him behind me. I knew that he was not the Angel of Death but the prophet Elijah.

"I hear Gad's footsteps," he said. "He's coming up the stairs."

"I HEAR Gad's footsteps," said Ilana, touching my arm. "He's coming up the stairs."

Slowly and with a blank look on his face Gad came into the room. Ilana ran toward him and kissed his lips, but gently he pushed her away.

"You stayed down there so long," she said. "What kept you?"

A cruel, sad smile crossed Gad's face.

"Nothing," he said. "I was watching him eat."

"He ate?" I asked in surprise. "You mean to say he was able to eat?"

"Yes, he ate," said Gad. "And with a good appetite, too."

I could not understand.

"What?" I exclaimed. "You mean to say he was hungry?"

"I didn't say he was hungry," Gad retorted. "I said he ate with a good appetite."

"So he wasn't hungry," I insisted.

Gad's face darkened.

"No, he wasn't hungry."

"Then why did he eat?"

"I don't know," said Gad nervously. "Probably to show me that he can eat even if he's not hungry."

Ilana scrutinized his face. She tried to catch his eye, but Gad was staring into space.

"What did you do after that?" she asked uneasily.

"After what?" said Gad brusquely.

"After he'd finished eating."

Gad shrugged his shoulders.

"Nothing," he said.

"What do you mean, *nothing*?"

"Nothing. He told me stories."

Ilana shook his arm.

"Stories? What kind of stories?"

Gad sighed in resignation.

"Just stories," he repeated, obviously tired of answering questions he considered grotesque.

I wanted to ask if he had laughed, if the hostage had got a laugh out of him. But I refrained. The answer could only have been absurd.

Gad's reappearance had roused Gideon and Joab from their sleep. With haggard faces they looked around the room, as if to assure themselves they weren't dreaming. Stifling a yawn, Joab asked Gad for the time.

"Four o'clock," said Gad, consulting his watch.

"So late? I'd never have thought it."

Gad beckoned to me to come closer.

"Soon it will be day," he observed.

"I know."

"You know what you have to do?"

"Yes, I know."

He took a revolver out of his pocket and handed it to me. I hesitated.

"Take it," said Gad.

The revolver was black and nearly new. I was afraid to even touch it, for in it lay all the whole difference between what I was and what I was going to be.

"What are you waiting for?" asked Gad impatiently. "Take it."

I held out my hand and took it. I examined it for a long time as if I did not know what purpose it could possibly serve. Finally I slipped it into my trouser pocket.

"I'd like to ask you a question," I said to Gad.

"Go ahead."

"Did he make you laugh?"

Gad stared at me coldly, as if he had not understood my question or the necessity for it. His brow was furrowed with preoccupation.

"John Dawson," I said. "Did he make you laugh?"

Gad's eyes stared through me; I felt them going through my head and coming out the other side. He must have been wondering what was going on in my mind, why I harped on this unimportant question, why I didn't seem to be suffering or to be masking my suffering or lack of suffering.

"No," he said at last; "he didn't make me laugh."

His own mask cracked imperceptibly. All his efforts were bent upon controlling the expression of his eyes, but he had neglected his mouth, and it was there that the crack showed. His upper lip betrayed bitterness and anger.

"How did you do it?" I asked in mock admiration. "Weren't his stories funny?"

Gad made a strange noise, not unlike a laugh. The silence that followed accentuated the sadness which an invisible hand had traced upon his lips.

"Oh, they were funny all right, very funny. But they didn't make me laugh."

He took a cigarette out of his shirt pocket, lit it, drew a few puffs and then, without waiting for me to ask anything more, went on:

"I was thinking of David, that's all."

I'll think of David too, I reflected. He'll protect me. John Dawson may try to make me laugh, but I won't do it. David will come to my rescue.

"It's getting late," said Joab, stifling another yawn.

The night was still looking in on us. But quite obviously it was getting ready to go away. I came to a sudden decision.

"I'm going down," I said.

"So soon?" said Gad, in a tone revealing either emotion or mere surprise. "You've got plenty of time. As much as an hour . . ."

I said that I wanted to go down before the time was up, to see the fellow, and talk, and get to know him. It was cowardly, I said, to kill a complete stranger. It was like war, where you don't shoot at men but into the night, and the wounded night emits cries of pain which are almost human. You shoot into the darkness, and you never know whether any of the enemy was killed, or which one. To execute a stranger would be the same thing. If I were to see him only as he died I should feel as if I had shot at a dead man.

This was the reason I gave for my decision. I'm not sure it was exact. Looking back, it seems to me that I was moved by curiosity. I had never seen a hostage before. I wanted to see a hostage who was doomed to die and who told funny stories. Curiosity or bravado? Perhaps a little of both . . .

"Do you want me to go with you?" asked Gad. A lock of hair had fallen over his forehead, but he did not push it back.

"No, Gad," I said. "I want to be alone with him."

Gad smiled. He was a commander, proud of his subaltern and expressing his pride in a smile. He laid his hand affectionately on my shoulder.

"Do you want someone to go with you?" asked the beggar.

"No," I repeated. "I'd rather be alone."

His eyes were immeasurably kind.

"You can't do it without them," he said, nodding his head in the direction of the crowd behind us.

"They can come later," I conceded.

The beggar took my head in his hands and looked into my eyes. His look was so powerful that for a moment I doubted my identity. I am that look, I said to myself. What else could I be? The beggar has many looks, and I am one of them. But his expression radiated kindness, and I knew that he could not regard kindly his own look. That was how my identity came back to me.

"Very well," he said; "they'll come later."

Now the boy, looking over the shadowy heads and bodies between us, offered to go with me. "Later," I said. My answer made him sad, but I could only repeat: "Later. I want to be alone with him."

"Good," said the child. "We'll come later."

I let my look wander over the room, hoping to leave it there and pick it up when I returned.

Ilana was talking to Gad, but he did not listen. Joab was yawning. Gideon rubbed his forehead as if he had a headache.

In an hour everything will be different, I reflected. I shan't see it the same way. The table, the chairs, the walls, the window, they will all have changed. Only the dead—my father and mother, the master and Yerachmiel—will be the same, for we all of us change together, in the same way, doing the same things.

I patted my pocket to make sure the revolver was still there. It was; indeed, I had the strange impression that it was alive, that its life was part of mine, that it had the same present and future destiny as myself. I was its destiny and it was mine. In an hour it too will have changed, I reflected.

"It's late," said Joab, stretching.

With my eyes I bade farewell to the room, to Ilana, to Gideon and his prayers, to Joab and his confused expression, to the table, the window, the walls, and the night. Then I went hurriedly into the kitchen as if I were going to my own execution. As I went down the stairs my steps slackened and became heavy.

J OHN DAWSON was a handsome man. In spite of his unshaven face, tousled hair, and rumpled shirt there was something distinguished about him.

He seemed to be in his forties—a professional soldier, no doubt—with penetrating eyes, a resolute chin, thin lips, a broad forehead, and slender hands.

When I pushed open the door I found him lying on a camp bed, staring up at the ceiling. The bed was the only piece of furniture in the narrow white cell. Thanks to an ingenious system of ventilation we had installed, the windowless cell was less stuffy than the open room above.

When he became aware of my presence John Dawson showed neither surprise nor fear. He did not get up but simply raised himself into a sitting position. He scrutinized me at length without saying a word, as if measuring the density of my silence. His stare enveloped my whole being and I wondered if he saw that I was a mass of eyes.

"What time is it?" he asked abruptly.

In an uncertain voice I answered that it was after four. He

frowned, as if in an effort to grasp the hidden meaning of my words.

"When is sunrise?" he said.

"In an hour," I answered. And I added, without knowing why: "Approximately."

We stared at each other for a long interval, and suddenly I realized that time was not moving at its normal, regular pace. In an hour I shall kill him, I thought. And yet I didn't really believe it. This hour which separates me from murder will be longer than a lifetime. It will belong, always, to the distant future; it will never be one with the past.

There was something age-old in our situation. We were alone not only in the cell but in the world as well, he seated, I standing, the victim and the executioner. We were the first—or the last—men of creation; certainly we were alone. And God? He was present, somewhere. Perhaps He was incarnate in the liking with which John Dawson inspired me. The lack of hate between executioner and victim, perhaps this is God.

We were alone in the narrow white cell, he sitting on the bed and I standing before him, staring at each other. I wished I could see myself through his eyes. Perhaps he was wishing he could see himself through mine. I felt neither hate nor anger nor pity; I liked him, that was all. I liked the way he scowled when he was thinking, the way he looked down at his nails when he was trying to formulate his thoughts. Under other circumstances he might have been my friend.

"Are you the one?" he asked abruptly.

How had he guessed it? Perhaps by his sense of smell. Death has an odor and I had brought it in with me. Or perhaps as soon as I came through the door he had seen that I had neither arms nor legs nor shoulders, that I was all eyes.

"Yes," I said.

I felt quite calm. The step before the last is the hard one; the last step brings clearheadedness and assurance.

"What's your name?" he asked.

This question disturbed me. Is every condemned man bound to ask it? Why does he want to know the name of his executioner? In order to take it with him to the next world? For what purpose? Perhaps I shouldn't have told him, but I could refuse nothing to a man condemned to die.

"Elisha," I said.

"Very musical," he observed.

"It's the name of a prophet," I explained. "Elisha was a disciple of Elijah. He restored life to a little boy by lying upon him and breathing into his mouth."

"You're doing the opposite," he said with a smile.

There was no trace of anger or hate in his voice. Probably he too felt clearheaded and assured.

"How old are you?" he asked with aroused interest.

Eighteen, I told him. For some reason I added: "Nearly nineteen."

He raised his head and there was pity on his thin, suddenly sharpened face. He stared at me for several seconds, then sadly nodded his head.

"I'm sorry for you," he said.

I felt his pity go through me. I knew that it would permeate me completely, that the next day I should be sorry for myself.

"Tell me a story," I said. "A funny one, if you can."

I felt my body grow heavy. The next day it would be heavier still, I reflected. The next day it would be weighed down by my life and his death, "I'm the last man you'll see before you die," I went on. "Try to make him laugh."

Once more I was enveloped by his look of pity. I wondered if everyone condemned to die looked at the last man he saw in the same way, if every victim pitied his executioner.

"I'm sorry for you," John Dawson repeated.

By dint of an enormous effort I managed to smile.

"That's no funny story," I remarked.

He smiled at me in return. Which of our two smiles was the sadder?

"Are you sure it isn't funny?"

No, I wasn't so sure. Perhaps there *was* something funny about it. The seated victim, the standing executioner—smiling, and understanding each other better than if they were childhood friends. Such are the workings of time. The veneer of conventional attitudes was wiped off; every word and look and gesture was naked truth instead of just one of its facets. There was harmony between us; my smile answered his; his pity was mine. No human being would ever understand me as he understood me at this hour. Yet I knew that this was solely on account of the roles that were imposed upon us. This was what made it a funny story.

"Sit down," said John Dawson, making room for me to his left on the bed.

I sat down. Only then did I realize that he was a whole head taller than I. And his legs were longer than mine, which did not even touch the ground.

"I have a son your age," he began, "but he's not at all like you. He's fair-haired, strong, and healthy. He likes to eat, drink, go to the pictures, laugh, sing, and go out with the girls. He has none of your anxiety, your unhappiness."

And he went on to tell me more about this son who was "studying at Cambridge." Every sentence was a tongue of flame which burned my body. With my right hand I patted the revolver in my pocket. The revolver too was incandescent, and burned my fingers.

I mustn't listen to him, I told myself. He's my enemy, and the enemy has no story. I must think of something else. That's why I wanted to see him, in order to think of something else while he was talking. Something else . . . but what? Of Ilana? Of Gad? Yes, I should think of Gad, who was thinking of David. I should think of our hero, David ben Moshe, who . . .

I shut my eyes to see David better, but to no purpose, because I had never met him. A name isn't enough, I thought. One must have a face, a voice, a body, and pin the name of David ben Moshe upon them. Better think of a face, a voice, a body that I actually knew. Gad? No, it was difficult to imagine Gad as a man condemned to die. Condemned to die . . . that was it. Why hadn't I thought of it before? John Dawson was condemned to die; why shouldn't I baptize him David ben Moshe? For the next five minutes you are David ben Moshe . . . in the raw, cold, white light of the death cell of the prison at Acre. There is a knock at the door, and the rabbi comes in to read the Psalms with you and hear you say the *Vidui*, that terrible confession in which you admit your responsibility not only for the sins you have committed, whether by word, deed, or thought, but also for those you may have caused others to commit. The rabbi gives you the traditional blessing: "The Lord bless you and keep you . . ." and exhorts you to have no fear. You answer that you are unafraid, that if you had a chance you would do the same thing all over. The rabbi smiles and says that everyone on the outside is proud of you. He is so deeply moved that he has to make a visible effort to hold back his tears; finally the effort is too much for him and he sobs aloud. But you, David, do not cry. You have tender feelings for the rabbi because he is the last man (the executioner and his assistants don't count) you will see before you die. Because he is sobbing you try to comfort him. "Don't cry," you say; "I'm not afraid. You don't need to be sorry for me."

"I'm sorry for you," said John Dawson. "*You* worry me, not my son."

He put his feet down on the floor. He was so tall that when he stood up he had to bend over in order not to bump his head against the ceiling. He put his hands in the pockets of his rumpled khaki trousers and began to pace up and down the cell: five steps in one direction, five in the other.

"That I admit is funny," I observed.

He did not seem to hear, but went on pacing from wall to wall. I looked at my watch; it was twenty past four. Suddenly he stopped in front of me and asked for a cigarette. I had a package of Players in my pocket and wanted to give them to him. But he refused to take the whole package, saying quite calmly that obviously he didn't have time to smoke them all.

Then he said with sudden impatience:

"Have you a pencil and paper?"

I tore several pages out of my notebook and handed them to him, with a pencil.

"Just a short note which I'd like to have sent to my son," he declared. "I'll put down the address."

I handed him the notebook to use as a pad. He laid the notebook on the bed and leaned over to write from a standing position. For several minutes the silence was broken only by the sound of the pencil running over the paper.

I looked down in fascination at his smooth-skinned hands with their long, slender, aristocratic fingers. With hands like those, I thought, it's easy to get along. There's no need to bow, smile, talk, pay compliments, or bring flowers. A pair of such hands do the whole job. Rodin would have liked to sculpt them . . .

The thought of Rodin made me think of Stefan, a German I

had known at Buchenwald. He had been a sculptor before the war, but when I met him the Nazis had cut off his right hand.

In Berlin, during the first years after Hitler came to power, Stefan and some of his friends organized an embryonic resistance group which the Gestapo uncovered shortly after its founding. Stefan was arrested, questioned, and subjected to torture. Give us names, they told him, and we will set you free. They beat and starved him, but he would not talk. Day after day and night after night they prevented him from sleeping, but still he did not give in. Finally he was haled before the Berlin chief of the Gestapo, a timid, mild man, who in a soft-spoken, fatherly manner, advised him to stop being foolishly stubborn. The sculptor heard him out in stony silence. "Come on," said the chief. "Give us just one name, as a sign of good will." Still Stefan would not speak. "Too bad," said the chief. "You're obliging me to hurt you."

At a sign from the chief two SS men led the prisoner into what looked like an operating room, with a dentist's chair installed near the window. Beside it, on a table with a white oilcloth cover, was an orderly array of surgical instruments. They shut the window, tied Stefan onto the chair and lit cigarettes. The mild-mannered chief came into the room, wearing a white doctor's jacket.

"Don't be afraid," he said; "I used to be a surgeon."

He puttered around with the instruments and then sat down in front of the prisoner's chair.

"Give me your right hand," he said. Studying it at close range, he added: "I'm told you're a sculptor. You have nothing to say? Well, I know it. I can tell from your hands. A man's hands tell a lot about him. Take mine, for instance. You'd never take them for a surgeon's hands, would you? The truth is that I never wanted to be a doctor. I wanted to be a painter or a musician. I never became one, but I still have the hands of an artist. Look at them."

"I looked at them, with fascination," Stefan told me. "He had the most beautiful, the most angelic hands I have ever seen. You would have sworn that they belonged to a sensitive, unworldly man."

"As a sculptor you need your hands," the Gestapo chief went on. "Unfortunately *we* don't need them," and so saying he cut off a finger.

The next day he cut off a second finger, and the day after that a third. Five days, five fingers. All five fingers of the right hand were gone.

"Don't worry," the chief assured him. "From a medical point of view, everything is in good order. There's no danger of infection."

"I saw him five times," Stefan told me. (For some inexplicable reason he was not killed but simply sent to a concentration camp.) "Every day for five days I saw him from very near by. And every time I could not take my eyes off those hands of his, the most beautifully shaped hands I had ever seen . . ."

John Dawson finished his note and held it out to me, but I hardly saw it. My attention was taken by his proud, smooth-skinned, frail hands.

"Are you an artist?" I asked him.

He shook his head.

"You've never painted or played a musical instrument, or at least wanted to do so?"

He scrutinized me in silence and then said dryly:

"No."

"Then perhaps you studied medicine."

"I never studied medicine," he said, almost angrily.

"Too bad."

"Too bad? Why?"

"Look at your hands. They're the hands of a surgeon. The kind of hands it takes to cut off fingers."

Deliberately he laid the sheets of paper on the bed.

"Is that a funny story?" he asked.

"Yes, very funny. The fellow who told it to me thought so. He used to laugh over it until he cried."

John Dawson shook his head and said in an infinitely sad voice:

"You hate me, don't you?"

I didn't hate him at all, but I wanted to hate him. That would have made it all very easy. Hate—like faith or love or war—justifies everything.

"Elisha, why did you kill John Dawson?"

"He was my enemy."

"John Dawson? Your enemy? You'll have to explain that better."

"Very well. John Dawson was an Englishman. The English were enemies of the Jews in Palestine. So he was my enemy."

"But Elisha, I still don't understand why you killed him. Were you his only enemy?"

"No, but I had orders. You know what that means."

"And did the orders make him your only enemy? Speak up, Elisha. Why did you kill John Dawson?"

If I had alleged hate, all these questions would have been spared me. Why did I kill John Dawson? Because I hated him, that's all. The absolute quality of hate explains any human action even if it throws something inhuman around it.

I certainly wanted to hate him. That was partly why I had come to engage him in conversation before I killed him. It was absurd reasoning on my part, but the fact is that while we were talking I hoped to find in him, or in myself, something that would give rise to hate.

A man hates his enemy because he hates his own hate. He says to himself: This fellow, my enemy, has made me capable of hate. I hate him not because he's my enemy, not because he hates me, but because he arouses me to hate.

John Dawson has made me a murderer, I said to myself. He has made me the murderer of John Dawson. He deserves my hate. Were it not for him, I might still be a murderer, but I wouldn't be the murderer of John Dawson.

Yes, I had come down to the cellar to feed my hate. It seemed easy enough. Armies and governments the world over have a definite technique for provoking hate. By speeches and films and other kinds of propaganda they create an image of the enemy in which he is the incarnation of evil, the symbol of suffering, the fountainhead of the cruelty and injustice of all times. The technique is infallible, I told myself, and I shall turn it upon my victim.

I did try to draw upon it. All enemies are equal, I said. Each one is responsible for the crimes committed by the others. They have different faces, but they all have the same hands, the hands that cut my friends' tongues and fingers.

As I went down the stairs I was sure that I would meet the man who had condemned David ben Moshe to death, the man who had killed my parents, the man who had come between me and the man I had wanted to become, and who was now ready to kill the man in me. I felt quite certain that I would hate him.

The sight of his uniform added fuel to my flames. There is nothing like a uniform for whipping up hate. When I saw his slender hands I said to myself: Stefan will carve out my hate for them. Again, when he bent his head to write the farewell note to his son, the son "studying at Cambridge," who liked to "laugh and go out with the girls," I thought: David is writing a last letter too, probably to the Old Man, before he puts his head in the hangman's noose. And when he talked, my heart went out to David, who had no one to talk to, except the rabbi. You can't talk to a rabbi, for he

75

is too concerned with relaying your last words to God. You can confess your sins, recite the Psalms or the prayers for the dead, receive his consolation or console him, but you can't talk, not really.

I thought of David whom I had never met and would never know. Because he was not the first of us to be hanged we knew exactly when and how he would die. At about five o'clock in the morning the cell door would open and the prison director would say: Get ready, David ben Moshe; the time has come. "The time has come," this is the ritual phrase, as if this and no other time had any significance. David would cast a look around the cell and the rabbi would say: "Come, my son." They would go out, leaving the cell door open behind them (for some reason no one ever remembers to close it) and start down the long passageway leading to the execution chamber. As the man of the hour, conscious of the fact that the others were there solely on his account, David would walk in the center of the group. He would walk with his head held high—all our heroes held their heads high—and a strange smile on his lips. On either side of the passageway a hundred eyes and ears would wait for him to go by, and the first of the prisoners to perceive his approach would intone the *Hatikva*, the song of hope. As the group advanced the song would grow louder, more human, more powerful, until its sound rivaled that of the footsteps . . .

When John Dawson spoke of his son I heard David's footsteps and the rising song. With his words John Dawson was trying to cover up the footsteps, to erase the sight of David walking down the passageway and the strange smile on his lips, to drown out the despairing sound of the *Hatikva*, the song of hope.

I wanted to hate him. Hate would have made everything so simple . . . Why did you kill John Dawson? I killed him because I hated him. I hated him because David ben Moshe hated him, and David ben Moshe hated him because he talked while he David was going down the somber passageway at whose far end he must meet his death.

"You hate me, Elisha, don't you?" John Dawson asked. There was a look of overflowing tenderness in his eyes.

"I'm trying to hate you," I answered.

"Why must you try to hate me, Elisha?"

He spoke in a warm, slightly sad voice, remarkable for the absence of curiosity.

Why? I wondered. What a question! Without hate, everything that my comrades and I were doing would be done in vain. Without hate we could not hope to obtain victory. Why do I try to hate you, John Dawson? Because my people have never known how to hate. Their tragedy, throughout the centuries, has stemmed from their inability to hate those who have humiliated and from time to time exterminated them. Now our only chance lies in hating you, in learning the necessity and the art of hate. Otherwise, John Dawson, our future will only be an extension of the past, and the Messiah will wait indefinitely for his deliverance.

"Why must you try to hate me?" John Dawson asked again.

"In order to give my action a meaning which may somehow transcend it."

Once more he slowly shook his head.

"I'm sorry for you," he repeated.

I looked at my watch. Ten minutes to five. Ten minutes to go. In ten minutes I should commit the most important and conclusive act of my life. I got up from the bed.

"Get ready, John Dawson," I said.

"Has the time come?" he asked.

"Very nearly," I answered.

He rose and leaned his head against the wall, probably in order to collect his thoughts or to pray or something of the kind.

Eight minutes to five. Eight minutes to go. I took the revolver out of my pocket. What should I do if he tried to take it from me? There was no chance of his escaping. The house was well guarded and there was no way of getting out of the cellar except through the kitchen. Gad, Gideon, Joab, and Ilana were on guard upstairs, and John Dawson knew it.

Six minutes to five. Six minutes to go. Suddenly I felt quite clearheaded. There was an unexpected light in the cell; the boundaries were drawn, the roles well defined. The time of doubt and questioning and uncertainty was over. I was a hand holding a revolver; I was the revolver that held my hand.

Five minutes to five. Five minutes to go.

"Have no fear, my son," the rabbi said to David ben Moshe. "God is with you."

"Don't worry, I'm a surgeon," said the mild-mannered Gestapo chief to Stefan.

"The note," John Dawson said, turning around. "You'll send it to my boy, won't you?"

He was standing against the wall; he was the wall. Three minutes to five. Three minutes to go.

"God is with you," said the rabbi. He was crying, but now David did not see him.

"The note. You won't forget, will you?" John Dawson insisted.

"I'll send it," I promised, and for some reason I added: "I'll mail it today."

"Thank you," said John Dawson.

David is entering the chamber from which he will not come out alive. The hangman is waiting for him. He is all eyes. David mounts the scaffold. The hangman asks him whether he wants his eyes banded. Firmly David answers no. A Jewish fighter dies with his eyes open. He wants to look death in the face.

Two minutes to five. I took a handkerchief out of my pocket, but John Dawson ordered me to put it back. An Englishman dies with his eyes open. He wants to look death in the face.

Sixty seconds before five o'clock. One minute to go.

Noiselessly the cell door opened and the dead trooped in, filling us with their silence. The narrow cell had become almost unbearably stuffy.

The beggar touched my shoulder and said:

"Day is at hand."

And the boy who looked the way I used to look said, with an uneasy expression on his face:

"This is the first time—" His voice trailed off, and then, as if remembering that he had left the sentence suspended he picked it up: "the first time I've seen an execution."

My father and mother were there too, and the grizzled master, and Yerachmiel. Their silence stared at me.

David stiffened and began to sing the *Hatikva*.

John Dawson smiled, with his head against the wall and his body as erect as if he were saluting a general.

"Why are you smiling?" I asked.

"You must never ask a man who is looking at you the reason for his smile," said the beggar.

"I'm smiling," said John Dawson, "because all of a sudden it has occurred to me that I don't know why I am dying." And after a moment of silence he added: "Do you?"

"You see?" said the beggar. "I told you that was no question to ask a man who is about to die."

Twenty seconds. This minute was more than sixty seconds long.

"Don't smile," I said to John Dawson. What I meant was: "I can't shoot a man who is smiling."

Ten seconds.

"I want to tell you a story," he said, "a funny story."

I raised my right arm.

Five seconds.

"Elisha—"

Two seconds. He was still smiling.

"Too bad," said the little boy. "I'd like to have heard his story."

One second.

"Elisha—" said the hostage.

I fired. When he pronounced my name he was already dead; the bullet had gone through his heart. A dead man, whose lips were still warm, had pronounced my name: *Elisha*.

He sank very slowly to the ground, as if he had slipped from the top of the wall. His body remained in a sitting position, with the head bowed down between the knees, as if he were still waiting to be killed. I stayed for a few moments beside him. There was a pain in my head and my body was growing heavy. The shot had left me deaf and dumb. That's it, I said to myself. It's done. I've killed. I've killed Elisha.

The ghosts began to leave the cell, taking John Dawson with them. The little boy walked at his side as if to guide him. I seemed to hear my mother say: "Poor boy! Poor boy!"

Then with heavy footsteps I walked up the stairs leading to the kitchen. I walked into the room, but it was not the same. The ghosts were gone. Joab was no longer yawning. Gideon was looking down at his nails and praying for the repose of the dead. Ilana lifted a sad countenance upon me; Gad lit a cigarette. They were silent, but their silence was different from the silence which all night long had weighed upon mine. On the horizon the sun was rising.

I went to the window. The city was still asleep. Somewhere a child woke up and began to cry. I wished that a dog would bark, but there was no dog anywhere nearby.

The night lifted, leaving behind it a grayish light the color of stagnant water. Soon there was only a tattered fragment of darkness, hanging in midair, the other side of the window. Fear caught my throat. The tattered fragment of darkness had a face. Looking at it, I understood the reason for my fear. The face was my own.